"IF YOU CARED ABOUT ME, YOU WOULDN'T ALWAYS BE ON THE RECEIVING END OF THIS RELATIONSHIP."

"What relationship?" She touched her glasses, then let her hand fall to her side. "I didn't think we—"

"Well, what *did* you think, Sylvie? That I had nothing better to do with my time? Didn't you consider that maybe, just maybe, I made time to be with you? You've never even admitted that you like having me around. It would be nice to hear you say it once in a while. A relationship has to be reciprocal, Sylvie."

"I told you in the beginning, I wasn't looking for a relationship, Max."

"And I said one just might find you anyway."

Her heart was beating so fast she could hardly think. "What did I say to that?"

Max rubbed a hand across his cheek. "I don't remember. What do you say now? What do you want from a relationship, Sylvie? With me?"

THAT SPECIAL SMILE

Karen Whittenburg

A CANDLELIGHT ECSTASY ROMANCE®

Published by
Dell Publishing Co., Inc.
1 Dag Hammarskjold Plaza
New York, New York 10017

ISBN: 0-440-18667-6

Printed in the United States of America

First printing—November 1985

*To DeAnn, my cousin, with love
and
To Roy,
who had the good fortune to marry her*

To Our Readers:

We have been delighted with your enthusiastic response to Candlelight Ecstasy Romances®, and we thank you for the interest you have shown in this exciting series.

In the upcoming months we will continue to present the distinctive, sensuous love stories you have come to expect only from Ecstasy. We look forward to bringing you many more books from your favorite authors and also the very finest work from new authors of contemporary romantic fiction.

As always, we are striving to present the unique, absorbing love stories that you enjoy most—books that are more than ordinary romance. Your suggestions and comments are always welcome. Please write to us at the address below.

Sincerely,

The Editors
Candlelight Romances
1 Dag Hammarskjold Plaza
New York, New York 10017

The first thing she noticed was the towel. It was an ordinary blue terry-cloth, slightly damp in places, but then so was the man who wore it draped casually around his waist. A drop of water hit the concrete porch and splattered on the tip of the soft kid leather of her Italian sandal in a cool bid for attention. Sylvie looked down. If the rest of him matched his feet, she thought, she would have a long way to look up.

She saw no need to hurry, though, and leisurely brought her gaze past hairy calves to muscled thighs, skipped the towel, and focused on the wet tangle of curls on his chest. Pursing her lips in an appraising frown, she lifted her eyes to a stubborn-looking chin, a mouth firmed with impatience, an almost-straight and not unattractive nose, narrowed eyes that were a cool blue—a deeper shade than the towel, she noted —dark brows, and ebony hair that gleamed with moisture.

Sylvie smiled. Now, who would have thought that a nice-looking, half-naked man would answer the door when *she* rang the bell?

"Good morning," she said easily. "You must be Max, although I was expecting someone . . . dryer."

One brow arched as he shifted his weight and adjusted the knot of the towel. "I would have been dryer, but someone was *leaning* on the doorbell." His voice was rich and deep and added a nuance of intimacy to the warm September morning.

Interesting, Sylvie decided, but then Juliette's conquests were always interesting in one way or another.

"I didn't think it worked," Sylvie explained cheerfully. "The way things have gone so far today, I thought there wasn't a chance in ten that you'd be here. Juliette told me if she was gone when I arrived to try your house next door."

The corners of his mouth tightened with a rueful frown. Men always smiled when Juliette's name was mentioned. It was a phenomenon Sylvie had observed many times before and had come to expect, but Max wasn't smiling. There wasn't even a hint of wistful affection in his eyes—they really were a gallant shade of blue—and she wondered if there was trouble in her sister's latest paradise.

Max rubbed a hand along the rough shadow of his jawline and dropped his gaze to the concrete and the ridiculously small, sandaled feet opposite his own. She had nice legs, although he couldn't help thinking they would be better served by a less dramatic mode of dress. From the tip of her high-heeled sandals to the fashionably padded shoulders of the green sheath she wore, to the round tortoiseshell glasses that framed wide, sea-green eyes, and the graceful curve of reddish-blond hair against her shoulders, she looked very Boston—and very much out of place on his front porch. This, of course, was Julie's much-touted, multitalented sister. What a hell of a way to begin the weekend, Max thought dryly.

"Your sister didn't happen to say what *I* might be able to do for you, did she?" His question was somewhat terse and won him a considering look.

"No, but I'm sure she knew you'd make me feel welcome." Sylvie's lips curved with just enough friendly warmth to soften any sting in her words. "Why would she have warned me that you make terrible coffee if she didn't believe you'd offer me a cup?"

Which, Max thought, pretty much put his options into perspective. "Well, if Julie told you to come over here, then by all means, come in." He invited her inside with a small sweep of his hand and stepped back, intending to vacate the doorway.

But Sylvie was a little too quick for him, and without knowing exactly how it happened, he found himself face to face with her, caught between the door and her more yielding form. There wasn't enough room in the narrow entrance for any degree of polite distance, and Max sensed that his guest wasn't the type to appreciate the humor—or any other positive aspect—of the unexpected closeness.

He retraced his step, but Sylvie obviously had the same idea, and their actions coincided again. This time, though, he felt the soft, rounded shape of her breasts against his chest and wasn't in such a hurry to dispel the sensation. After all, she was the one who had rung the doorbell.

Sylvie lifted her chin and met his gaze. "I believe we need a plan of action here."

"I could suggest one."

"Oh, please, allow me." With a haughty sort of confidence she placed her hand flat on the center of his bare chest and held him in place until she had moved past him into the house.

No, Max decided as he followed and closed the door behind him, she definitely did not appreciate the possibilities of the situation.

"Would you like a cup of coffee?" he asked with what he considered admirable charm under the circumstances.

She turned from her curious perusal of the front room. "Is it as bad as Juliette said?" Sylvie's smile appeared then, surprising him with its open sincerity. "No, I'm sure it couldn't be. Considering the awful stuff my sister calls coffee, I have to give you the benefit of the doubt."

If this was any indication of the way the conversation would run, Max thought, he would probably need a little caffeine himself. "Is that a yes or a no, Sylvie Anne?"

"Sylvie," she corrected, "and, yes."

"What?"

"Yes, thank you, I'd love to have a cup of coffee and my name is Sylvie." She pronounced each word crisply, as if she meant business.

Max eyed her speculatively. "But Julie calls you Sylvie Anne."

"As my younger sister she feels entitled to call me a number of things. But I only use my middle name in extreme emergencies, and so far, in twen—" She closed her lips around the revelation and kept her age to herself. There were certain things a man had no business knowing about a woman. "So far, there hasn't been an emergency that extreme."

Max felt an irrelevant amusement nudging his irritation as he observed her from a prudent distance.

She was twenty-nine, moving in on thirty. Julie had told him. So, he thought, there was at least one Achilles' heel in Sylvie's aura of perfect composure. His frustration with this interruption in his day took a subtle turn toward discovery. Maybe, with the right approach, he could salvage his sense of humor and still manage to enjoy the morning. After all, he'd done worse things on a Saturday morning than entertaining an attractive, albeit presumptuous, redhead.

Sylvie tapped one restless foot and wondered why Max was staring at her with the hint of a smile hovering about his mouth. He certainly seemed relaxed for a man who was wearing nothing more than a towel in front of a complete stranger. She touched the tortoiseshell rim of her glasses, settling them more securely on the bridge of her nose and thereby settling her own oddly ambivalent feelings about his lack of appropriate attire.

"If you want to change towels or something, I'll be glad to get the coffee for myself. Just point me toward the kitchen."

His jaw tightened. Max had been about to make the same suggestion, but it annoyed him out of all proportion that *she* had done so. Sylvie Anne was very pushy for an uninvited guest, and he'd be damned if he'd let her make herself at home, regardless of how self-conscious he felt wrapped from waist to mid-thigh in damp terry cloth.

"I'll get the coffee," he said, motioning her toward the sofa as he moved toward the doorway and the kitchen beyond. "You can wait here. Just make yourself—" he caught the "at home" as it was about to escape—"comfortable. I'll be back in a minute." Max pushed the swinging doors apart and entered the kitchen.

Sylvie sank onto the sofa, feeling a bit out of sorts with the greeting she'd received. Why hadn't Juliette stayed home this morning? Sylvie wondered, sighing with the knowledge that there would be an explanation. Not a reasonable one, of course, but Juliette always had an explanation. With a rueful look at her surroundings Sylvie came to the conclusion that she should have accepted Juliette's offer to meet her at the airport in Little Rock.

But if she had, she might still be waiting there. On top of that she'd be dependent on her sister's pedal-to-the-metal method of driving during the entire length of her stay. No, Sylvie reaffirmed her original decision as the only sane course of action. It was better that she'd made arrangements to lease a car, and the trip from Little Rock hadn't actually been that bad. If only Juliette could, just once, be where she was supposed to be when she was supposed to be there. Maybe Max had a key to Juliette's house . . . ?

The thought trailed into futile wishing. Juliette had lived in Eureka Springs, Arkansas, for almost five months now. If she had ever given Max a key to her house, she would long since have borrowed it back and forgotten to return it to him. Juliette was forever locking herself out, even in on occasion.

Sylvie gently rubbed her cheek with a fingertip, absently checked the fit of her glasses, and relaxed against the rough-woven fabric of the sofa. Her gaze circled the room once and then again, looking for something. Information, she supposed. Little details about Max McConnell that Juliette might have forgotten to mention, as impossible as that was to believe. In the past few weeks the telephone wires between Boston and Eureka Springs had hummed with his name.

Now that she'd met him, though, she had to admit a certain amount of curiosity. He wasn't at all what she'd expected, nothing like the men Juliette usually fell for. Physically, there were no standards. Juliette showed no prejudice against or preference for any certain height, weight, or eye color. But Sylvie had a vague idea that Max's basic philosophy was different from that of most of the men Juliette had dated, and he certainly seemed to possess a more casual attitude than the men she herself knew. Sylvie searched her memory and couldn't think of anyone in her acquaintance, male or female, who would have answered the door wearing a towel.

But Max had done so. And he hadn't shown even a respectable degree of embarrassment. In fact, he'd motioned her inside and then tried to hold her hostage in the doorway, watching her throughout as if he thought the whole incident had been *her* fault. Crossing her ankles, Sylvie smoothed the pageboy cut of her hair and then began tracing a fingertip over her palm, remembering the warm, rough texture of his chest and the faint rhythm of his heartbeat beneath her touch.

Max was a large man, and if pressed into honesty, Sylvie knew she would have to admit that he had a certain amount of physical appeal. She could understand Juliette's attraction. Max was worth a second look, even when he was dripping wet. He wasn't *her* type, of course, but then she was very particular.

She examined a tiny nick in the polished sheen of

one oval fingernail, glad that she was no longer impressed by brawn and muscle. She was past all that nonsense. On her twenty-seventh birthday she had decided her life was full and happy without a man and she had simply stopped looking for Mr. Right. It had been surprisingly easy, perhaps because her past experiences with men never had been especially satisfying. Over the years most of the men she had felt a strong attraction to had considered her merely a good friend and confidante, but the men from whom she wanted only friendship seemed intent on sweeping her off her feet.

Someday, someone . . . Sylvie had heard those words too many times to be fooled and she had long since accepted that marriage and motherhood were not in her future. It didn't even matter anymore. She wasn't sure it ever really had. She was happy. She liked being independent and she didn't think about what she might be missing, except once in a great while when it occurred to her to wonder what it might be like to share life, liberty, and the pursuit of happiness—maybe even a faded blue bath-towel—with a man. But she never wondered long.

A muffled sound of frustration came from the kitchen and a wry smile settled on her lips. Max was probably wishing her a dozen miles away. It really was rather gauche of her to impose on him this way. Still, she had wanted to meet him, and she had thought he would be delighted to have the opportunity to quiz her about Juliette.

In the past Sylvie had counseled a number of prospective suitors for Juliette's affections. It had been annoying at times, entertaining at others, but she hadn't minded; it was just a part of being Juliette's older sister. Besides, Sylvie felt it contributed a sense of objectivity and humor to her own view of love and its inevitable stages.

The thought of counseling Max McConnell was amusing. He didn't seem to be the type of man who would ask questions about baby Juliette and how she grew, but Sylvie knew he would. Every man did at one time or another. The bigger they were, the harder they fell; Max must have taken a real tumble. He was probably in the kitchen at that very moment planning how to broach the subject.

There was a clatter of china against china as Max pushed open the swinging doors and backed carefully into the living room. In each hand he balanced a cup and saucer, and he was dressed. Sylvie scanned the long length of his muscled legs, covered now in faded denim. His feet were still bare, but she imagined he hadn't had time to do more than pull on the jeans and the loose, unbuttoned flannel shirt he wore. Maybe he had realized somewhat belatedly that he was underdressed for the occasion. To her way of thinking he still was.

"Thank you, Max. The coffee smells wonderful." She took the cup he held out to her and brought it to her lips for a first, nearly scalding, sip. "Mmm, not bad. I'm glad you found time to put on some clothes."

His cup clanked against the saucer as he looked at her in surprise. "Were you worried?"

"Only about your health. Juliette would never forgive me if you took cold."

"Rest easy, Sylvie Anne. I won't hold you responsible and I'm sure Juliette won't either."

Sylvie took another sip of coffee and watched as he

seated himself in a chair opposite the sofa. "I'll keep up the premiums on my insurance, just the same."

"That's always a good idea." He balanced the saucer on the wide stuffed arm of his chair, set the cup on top of it, and decided to try a simple, straightforward question. "How long will you be visiting Julie?"

"I'll be here all winter, until the middle of March."

"March?" he repeated slowly. "But that's six months."

"Yes," Sylvie agreed with a droll smile at his distressed tone. "Do you think I'll need a visitor's permit?"

"No, but you might want to take up a hobby. There isn't much to do here during the winter. Shops close, people leave, and it gets quiet. Very quiet. We also get some dandy snowfalls. I guess you're used to cold weather, though, since you live up north. Boston, isn't it?"

"Boston it is." Sylvie dropped her gaze to the steam rising from her coffee cup. Max didn't appear to be thrilled at the prospect of her lengthy visit. He probably was envisioning her in the role of unwanted chaperone to him and his Juliette. Ah, well, he'd get over that misconception soon enough, and for now it wouldn't hurt for him to show her a measure of respect.

"Are you one of the residents who leave?" she asked. "Or do you like the cold, quiet Arkansas winters?"

"Sometimes," he answered, leaving room for choice, and then, she was sure, he deliberately changed the subject. "I understand from Julie that you're an insurance investigator. She told me you have your own agency."

"I am and I do. Smith-Kessler does claim investigations for many of the larger insurance companies."

"And how does the Kessler half of the business feel about your extended visit to Arkansas?" Max kept his lips in a polite curve, although it required some effort.

"Phillip thought it was a wonderful idea. Of course, he thinks everything is wonderful these days." As she set aside her cup, Max noticed her pause and the soft shadow of affection that touched her mouth. "Phillip, my business associate," she explained, "is newly married to someone he met while working on an art forgery case last winter. Elleny is delightful and her son, A. J., has the charm of Tom Sawyer. I've never seen Phillip happier or more dedicated to sticking around the home office."

"So you decided to take a leave of absence and give yourself some time to adjust to the idea that he's married." It was a casual comment, born, he supposed, of the bits of information Julie had given him from time to time and spoken aloud simply to avoid an awkward silence. But Max knew the moment her gaze pinned him that he'd surprised Sylvie. No, he decided, it was more than that. For one brief instant he'd caught her unaware, glimpsing a touch of vulnerability beneath her assertive composure. For reasons he didn't quite understand, Max decided to press the issue and see what she'd say. "Or is it your heart that has to make the adjustment?"

Sylvie had no intention of answering, regardless of her momentary discomposure. She didn't know how Max had come up with such an idea, but it was disconcerting to think he was that perceptive. She wasn't really in love with Phillip; it had always been just a wistful fancy, a harmless fantasy she'd entertained on occasion. She'd known from their first meeting that Phillip would never be seriously interested in her, but sometimes she'd imagined what it would be like if he were. It was one thing, however, for *her* to imagine it and quite another for a total stranger to question her about it.

She raised her brows in cool warning, even as a throaty ripple of laughter parted her lips. "Ah, you're a romantic. I never would have suspected it, Max, from the things Juliette's told me about you." Sylvie shrugged in delicate amusement. "You can believe I'm here to recover from a broken heart, if you like. But actually the reason is much more mundane. The business is doing quite well, and since Phillip is there to manage it, I decided this was as good a time as any to take a leave of absence and help Juliette get her dress shop started."

Max nodded, silently applauding Sylvie's performance. If not for that moment of hesitation he might have believed her. He didn't really *care* what sort of relationship she had with her business partner, he told himself, but he did find her reaction interesting. He got the distinct impression that Sylvie placed herself above such a simple human failing as falling in love, and he couldn't help thinking that someone needed to give her pedestal a good shake just to remind her she was mortal too. He smiled to himself, glad that that particular responsibility was not his.

"Ah, yes," he said, returning his thoughts to the subject at hand. "Julie's dress shop."

Sylvie didn't like the timbre of laughter in his voice, and she didn't much care for the say he kept looking at her. "Has she talked to you about it?"

"Practically nonstop."

"Her enthusiasm *is* a little overwhelming at times, isn't it?" Sylvie smiled.

Max, once again caught off guard by her smile, paused before replying. "I guess you must share some of that enthusiasm if you're willing to spend the winter in Eureka Springs. After the tourist season the town really shuts down."

He kept coming back to that, Sylvie thought. Was he hoping to scare her away with threats of boredom? "I never have trouble staying busy," she replied, "and there will be dozens of details involved in getting the shop ready to open by spring."

"Julie said you're good with details."

Sylvie saw no reason to deny it. "I am."

Max saw no reason to pursue the conversation. Sylvie Anne was beginning to live up to his expectations: a paragon of talents and virtue. Perfectly groomed, perfectly polite, and perfectly unexciting —except for her smile. He wondered where Juliette might be and when she might return. And he wondered what he could do to get rid of his unexpected guest. Placing his cup on the table beside the chair, he glanced up and caught Sylvie watching him.

She didn't look away. Neither did he. Her eyes really were green, he thought. He'd noticed their color before, of course, but only in a cursory manner and not with the usual attention to detail that was so essential to his work. So few people actually had green eyes. Usually, the shade was more hazel or gray, but not a true color. Intrigued, he leaned forward, letting his gaze shift to her hair and its burnished contrast against her creamy skin. She was lovely, he silently admitted. Her outer sophistication didn't quite match a certain winsome quality in her smile, and the large glasses somehow lent a vulnerability to her appearance that he was sure she wasn't aware of.

She lifted a hand to adjust the glasses and Max wondered if it was a nervous gesture. He thought it might be and felt curiously pleased at the idea that she was unsettled by his observant gaze. He smiled. So did she . . . and an odd sensation skimmed his nerve endings and warmed them to active awareness. Of all things, he was beginning to find her very attractive. And a bit of a challenge.

"At the risk of interrupting your concentration," she said, "would you mind if I had another cup of coffee?"

Max didn't stir; neither did he alter his concentration by any appreciable degree. Some mischievous impulse urged him to test her sense of humor. "You have very unusual eyes, Sylvie Anne."

"My ophthalmologist tells me the same thing. You should try to be a bit more original with your compliments, Max." She lifted her shoulder in a perky shrug. "And if you truly want to win my support, you'll stop using my middle name."

Win her support? He didn't know what she meant, but he wasn't sure he wanted to ask. Sylvie just might be more of a challenge than he was prepared to tackle. "Why don't I just get you a refill?" He rose and came toward her.

"Thank you, Max." Sylvie extended her cup and allowed herself a moment to enjoy the crease that amusement had etched in his left cheek. It wasn't a dimple, he was too ruggedly masculine for that, it was a slight indentation in an otherwise lean face, and Sylvie felt a ripple of interest in a secluded corner of her heart. Phillip had told her once that if she ever found a man who could talk to her for longer than ten minutes without getting a crazed look in his eyes, she should handcuff him and take him home to meet her family.

When Max took the mug and left the room, Sylvie couldn't resist checking her watch. Seventeen minutes and still counting. That was, of course, if he didn't duck out the back door. Somehow she knew he wasn't the type. Besides, he hadn't asked a single question yet about Juliette. Funny, she'd have pegged him as a man who got right to the point instead of wasting time trying to gain her support for his romance with her sister. Did he really think she had that much influence over Juliette's heart? Even if she had, she wouldn't interfere. Especially since Juliette had far more experience with such things than she herself did. But Max didn't know that, and she certainly wasn't about to tell him.

When Max returned, Sylvie took the cup and saucer from his outstretched hand, murmured a polite appreciation, and cast a surreptitious glance at his expression. His eyes were clear, his smile even. But for reasons she couldn't begin to explain, she felt uneasy. Tucking a strand of shoulder-length hair behind her ear, she grabbed the first random thought that crossed her mind.

"Don't tell me, Max. Let me guess," she said in a considering tone as she watched him settle into the chair again. "I'll bet you played running back."

His brows arched in surprise. "Football, you mean?" He shook his head and laughed deep in his throat. "No, mostly I played running scared. I've never understood why anyone would want to risk bone, tendon, and brain dysfunction for a sport."

"It has a lot to do with money, I believe."

"Only for a chosen few. At any rate, I knew there had to be a healthier way to earn a college scholarship."

"And did you?"

"Did I what? Earn a scholarship?" He gave her a lazy smile. "Yes. Academic. Does that impress you?"

She didn't know quite what to make of his disparaging tone. "Yes," she answered. "But then, I'm easily impressed by intelligence. And I also happen to know how difficult it is to get a scholarship. That's the only way I was able to attend Southern Methodist University."

He nodded and shifted to a more comfortable, more casual position in the chair. "Yes, I know. Julie told me all about it, from orientation right through your magna cum laude graduation."

"I think Juliette has spent far too much time talking about me."

After a few moments it became apparent that Max wasn't going to argue the point, and Sylvie decided to give the conversation a new direction. "She's certainly spent a lot of time lately talking about you."

There. His eyebrows rose at that information. "Really? What does she say about me?"

Sylvie had known he would get around to asking that question eventually, but she hadn't expected to have to prod him into it. She prepared to answer him, but as she parted her lips, Max interrupted with a laughing smile.

"No, on second thought, don't tell me. It would only embarrass both of us."

Somehow Sylvie didn't think so. "I doubt that, Max. Juliette has said some very nice things about you."

"Yes, I'm sure she has, but I believe we can find a more interesting topic to pass the time." Max allowed a subtle dare to insinuate itself into his voice. "Why don't we talk about you, Sylvie Anne?"

"There are so many reasons, I couldn't begin to name them. And speaking of names, I'll remind you —again—that mine consists of only two syllables, not three."

"I'll try to remember." Max lifted the coffee cup to his lips and drank, wondering why she was so defensive about her name. Maybe she didn't feel it meshed with her proper image. "I suppose I could think of a nickname for you."

Her green eyes became openly skeptical, as if she recognized he was teasing but was disinclined to acknowledge it. "I hardly think that would be worth your while, Max. After all, we're only going to be neighbors."

"That's an easily corrected detail."

"I suppose so. But I'd hate for you to feel you had to move away for six months."

He laughed then, a low, husky appreciation for her dry humor. There might be hope for her yet, he thought. "I meant, Sylvie, that we could become more than neighbors."

"You think *that's* an 'easily corrected detail'?"

The cool doubt in her tone clenched his sudden determination. In that instant Max made up his mind to become more than just a neighbor to Sylvie. A friend, perhaps, or maybe something more. And he would do it if only because such supreme confidence as Sylvie's deserved to be tested.

"Oh, I'm sure of it," he replied smoothly. "Providing, of course, that one of us was inclined to correct it." Max leaned back, confident that the winter was going to be entertaining, if nothing else. He smiled.

A suspicious warmth began in the pit of her stomach, but Sylvie dismissed it as an inappropriate response. She didn't like parlor games and she was beginning to think she didn't like Max McConnell either.

"Providing, of course," she paraphrased him, right down to the playful arch of her eyebrows, "that one of us could be persuaded it was worth correcting."

His pause was strictly for effect. "Point well taken, Sylvie A— Sylvie. But don't worry, I'm hardly ever unreasonable."

"Just unreasoned," she murmured into her coffee cup.

Amusement pulled at his lips and he didn't resist the laughter that welled up inside him. "I suppose only time will tell."

Her lips curved at that, but just barely. She had no idea why he was flirting with her, but she had no doubt that that was exactly what he was doing. Perhaps it was time she reintroduced her sister's name into the conversation.

"Juliette tells me you've lived here for a number of years."

"That's true."

"And Juliette said you have a shop downtown."

"On Spring Street."

"What kind of shop?"

"You mean Juliette didn't tell you?" His voice

dropped to a soft bass and his eyes twinkled a seductive blue.

The curious warmth in her stomach curled tighter and Sylvie found it more difficult to ignore this time. What could Max possibly hope to gain by this kind of behavior?

"Juliette said you have a toy store."

"She's right." His smile deepened. "Was she right when she told me there's no special man in your life?"

"Why would she tell you something like that?"

"Because I asked. Is it true?"

"That, Max, is none of your business."

"Yet."

She held the saucer tighter and regarded him suspiciously. But he noticed the way she used her other hand to adjust her glasses and congratulated himself on his perception. Impulsive and foolhardy it would undoubtedly prove to be, but at least his strategy was getting a response.

"I don't believe you and I could reach that point of familiarity in six *years*, much less six months," she said coolly, unable—or unwilling?—to understand how a complete stranger could elicit such a strong reaction from her.

He shrugged. "You could be right, Sylvie, but as I said before, winters here can be long and lonely."

"Which only proves you've never spent a winter next door to Juliette," she said, setting her coffee aside.

The crease made a fleeting reappearance in his cheek. "Or Juliette's sister."

Her restless fingers drummed in silent annoyance against the sofa arm. She was beginning to suspect the motivation for this all-out flirtation, and she didn't like the possibility at all. Part of her wanted to tell him exactly what she thought of him, but another part simply wanted to laugh at the complete nonsense he was dishing out. She chose a more middle-of-the-road approach.

"You don't seem to care what Juliette might think, Max."

His forehead wrinkled with a frown. "Well, no, I can't say I've given it a great deal of thought. Is that a requirement?"

"A requirement for what?"

"For getting to know you better." He relaxed against the back of the chair, stretched his legs out, halfway across the carpet it seemed, and crossed one sockless ankle over the other. It was a very casual posture and she resented it. He could at least sit up straight and keep his feet out of the middle of the floor while he flirted with her.

"I don't believe you know my sister very well, Max."

He looked surprised and suddenly just a bit serious. "You could be right."

"I am. And I'm going to do you a favor and give you fair warning that you'll never make Juliette jealous by flirting with me. Or anyone else, for that matter. She's not the jealous type."

His bewildered expression was a masterpiece of its kind. And then he chuckled, a quiet sound, a throaty ripple of laughter that wrapped a warm contentment about her heart and made her wish, for a fleeting second, that she could laugh with him.

"And what would you say, Sylvie Anne, if I told you I have no ulterior motive in flirting with you?"

"I would say you'd be in a no-win situation." She reached for the coffee cup that sat neglected on the table beside her.

Her challenge didn't appear to faze him, except to alter his amusement to a full grin. "You're absolutely right. Either way, it wouldn't be very flattering to you, would it?"

She put the cup back without bringing it anywhere near her lips. Juliette was right. He made terrible coffee. "Nor you, Max."

"Then I may as well have ulterior motives, don't you think?"

"What I think doesn't seem to matter to you, so you should suit yourself. And while you do that, I'll go back to Juliette's house and wait for her there." Sylvie tucked her purse under the crook of her arm and rose.

Max got to his feet in easy acceptance of her decision. "You might as well stay," he said, as if it didn't matter much to him either way. "I'll fix more coffee."

"No, thank you."

Max intentionally stepped close to Sylvie, closer than was necessary for a friendly good-bye. He half expected her to plant the spike of her heel somewhere in the middle of his foot, but instead she lifted her chin and, in one concise movement, adjusted those outlandish glasses against the bridge of her nose.

He couldn't remember the last time he'd been so intrigued with so little encouragement. Something about Sylvie appealed to his romantic instincts. Or maybe it was his sense of adventure that was leading him God knew where. Or could it be, he wondered, as simple as a purely physical attraction?

"If you don't mind?"

Her words were pointed, and although Sylvie kept them dangerously soft, she didn't let him see any sign of discomfiture—if there *was* any to see. But he sensed that she wasn't as unaffected by his nearness as she'd like him to believe, or as she'd like to believe herself. But that, he reasoned with a wry smile, was what made her interesting.

"Not at all." He led the way to the front door and made a point of keeping his distance as she opened the door and stepped outside. "Are you sure you don't want to wait here, Sylvie Anne?"

"Absolutely sure." She turned, hesitated as if weighing preference against etiquette, and then extended her hand for his handshake. "It's been very nice to meet you, Max. The coffee was . . . memorable." Her gaze swept over him and her accompanying smile was genuinely amused. "Juliette, obviously, has no taste."

He took her hand and cradled it in his palm. "Well, I'm glad *you* appreciate the finer things in life, Sylvie. Come share my caffeine anytime."

"That's very generous, Max. Maybe sometime before I leave, I'll be able to have coffee with you again." Her smile faded a bit as she flexed her hand and realized he wasn't ready to let go.

"Oh, I'm sure we'll be seeing a lot of each other, Sylvie Anne."

Not if she could do anything to prevent it, Sylvie decided. She had already seen all she wanted to see of Max McConnell. "Well, thanks again."

His fingers closed over hers and his thumb sketched a lazy circle on the back of her hand. "It was my pleasure."

For one brief second she enjoyed the caress and the fragile thread of an awakening perception that coursed through her. Then she took charge of the handshake and her hand was her own again. The blast of a car horn at that moment was the sweetest sound she'd heard in days.

"Juliette's home," she announced unnecessarily as she stepped back and away from him. "We couldn't have timed that better, could we?"

Max was sure he could have timed it better with his wristwatch tied behind his back. But as he watched Sylvie walk toward the tiny foreign car that Juliette drove, he decided it wouldn't hurt to spend a little time considering the consequences of the morning. He should, but he probably wouldn't. Sylvie wasn't like anyone he'd ever met—she wasn't even like anyone he'd ever read about. But he had a feeling. . . .

Leaning his shoulder against the doorjamb, Max watched the sisters exchange greetings and welcoming hugs. There was a certain amount of family resemblance between the two, he supposed, although it wasn't striking. Where Juliette's hair was summer blond, Sylvie's was autumn gold. Sylvie was taller than her sister, but not by much. And where Juliette was undeniably curvy, Sylvie was, well, more subdued, Max finally decided. There were other differences, of course, but he already knew that appearance was the least of them.

He could see grocery sacks through the passenger window of the sports car. How typical of Julie to plan for her sister's visit weeks in advance and then wait until the morning of her arrival to buy groceries.

Max shook his head. Apparently, Sylvie was laboring under the mistaken assumption that he was enamored of her sister. He didn't know how he'd managed to keep from groaning aloud when she'd accused him of flirting with her to make Juliette jealous. There was no way of knowing what Julie might have said to give Sylvie the wrong impression. After all, Julie said so very many things.

Sylvie, on the other hand, was more cautious. She was worlds removed from Julie's delightful, but tiring, zaniness. That in itself, he supposed, could be reason enough for this inexplicable attraction he was feeling. But Max didn't really think his newly awakened interest was rooted in shallow challenges. There was more to it than that. He raised his hand in answer to Juliette's wave; then his eyes sought Sylvie and watched her carry a sack of groceries toward the house.

Sylvie Anne. Max turned all three syllables over in his mind. An interesting name, an intriguing woman.

Not such a bad way to begin the weekend, after all, he thought with a smile as he turned and went inside.

CHAPTER TWO

"Didn't I tell you, Sylvie? Isn't he absolutely . . ." The sentence dwindled into an optional ending, as Juliette's sentences so often did.

From a ladder-back chair beside the kitchen table Sylvie watched her sister put groceries into cupboards and refrigerator.

"I couldn't *believe* it when I found out he lived next door." With a shake of her short blond curls Juliette lifted the carton of milk and held it against her lavender T-shirt as she balanced eggs, cheese, bacon, and a can of ready-made biscuits in her arms. "Honestly, who would ever have thought *I* could be so lucky?"

Sylvie sighed for the third time in fifteen minutes, which was approximately how long she'd been with Juliette. "The thought certainly never entered *my* mind," she said dryly. "But then I know what terrible luck you've always enjoyed when it comes to men."

Juliette wrinkled her nose at her sister's sarcasm and then giggled with her usual irrepressible delight. "And I always do enjoy it."

It was no less than the truth, and Sylvie had to smile. She sometimes wondered if her sister had any idea that thousands of women went days, even weeks, at a time without meeting any interesting men.

"But this time"—Juliette paused for an instant while she carefully added a small container of taco dip to her cache—"why, the chances of moving next door to a man like Max . . ." She turned and took two steps to the refrigerator door, which Sylvie rose to open. "My God, Sylvie, he's even single!"

"Which should have been your first clue, Juliette." Sylvie moved back to the table in the center of her sister's small red-and-white kitchen. She surveyed the remaining groceries and the cabinets, trying to match one with the other. "No man reaches the age of thirty-five single, unattached, and self-supporting, without either intending to continue in that state or being unable to persuade some unsuspecting female into helping him change it." She looked dubiously at a can of ready-to-serve gravy mix before tucking it into the cabinet above the sink. Out of sight, out of mind. "And from my limited observation," she continued, "I don't think your neighbor could charm his way out of a rain barrel."

Juliette straightened and stepped back to let the refrigerator door close. "Well, Max certainly made an impression on you, didn't he? What on earth did he do to win such a forceful response?"

"He didn't do anything. I just didn't care for his casual attitude about things."

Bracing a hand against the counter top, Juliette tilted her head to one side and her blue eyes became mildly appraising. "What things?"

Sylvie stood on tiptoe to push a package onto the top shelf. "Oh, his clothing, for one."

"I guess that means he wasn't wearing a suit and

tie," Juliette replied with a touch of sarcasm. "Sylvie, when are you going to stop believing that 'real' men wear only pinstripes?"

Sylvie's frown came from years of experience in dealing with a sassy younger sister. "I happen to like the way a man looks in a suit, pinstripe or any other tasteful fabric. It's a personal preference and has nothing to do with your neighbor, who, as a matter-of-fact, answered his door wearing terry cloth."

"What?" Juliette's surprise was wrapped in laughter as she took a step toward the table. "You saw Max McConnell in his *robe?*"

"No, he was wearing a towel." The memory flashed unbidden through her mind and only served to renew her opinion. Restless beneath her sister's assessing regard, Sylvie began putting away the remaining groceries. "You certainly bought enough food, Juliette. Is this a normal restocking of shelves or are we preparing for winter?"

"I just realized this morning that the cupboards were getting bare and I didn't know if you'd be hungry when you got here, so I ran to the store," Juliette said in a soft, absentminded way.

Sylvie knew the subject of terry cloth was not forgotten, and she made a stab at redirecting the conversation. "You could have waited for me. I called you from Fayetteville as soon as the plane landed and told you I was renting the first available car. It's only an hour-and-a-half drive. Did you think I was going to get lost along the way?"

Juliette sat in the chair Sylvie had vacated and pursed her lips thoughtfully. "You're very touchy, Sylvie Anne. But I suppose the sight of Max McConnell in a towel would upset my equilibrium too." Her hesitation was just long enough to accommodate an exasperating grin. "Was it a very *big* towel, Sylvie?"

"Big enough, Juliette. And I'm sure any touchiness on my part can be attributed to yesterday's flight from Boston, an overnight stay in Little Rock, and this morning's flight—I use the term loosely—to Fayetteville." Smoothing her hair with a fingertip stroke, Sylvie anchored the strands behind her ear and adjusted her glasses. "I don't think I've ever flown quite so close to the ground. Either the pilot was nearsighted or he's moonlighting as a crop duster."

"But you're here." Juliette kicked off a shoe and wiggled her toes. "And I am glad. Do you know how long it's been since we had more than a few days at a time to spend together? Even last Christmas at Dad's, we had less than a week to catch up on everything."

Sylvie laughed. "And we had to repeat every other word. I don't understand why Dad won't wear his hearing aid."

"Probably for the same reason you won't wear your contact lenses, too much trouble."

No, Sylvie thought, that was not her reason at all. "How soon do I get the grand tour of the new dress shop?"

"As soon as you get the groceries put away." Juliette's smile was teasing and eager. "Wait until you see it. Honestly, Syl, Hannah Lee House is the most wonderful example of Victorian architecture. And I got such a good buy. Of course, even with the money I inherited from Mother, I wouldn't have had enough if you hadn't agreed to invest in the idea."

"I'm just glad you asked." It wasn't a total lie, Sylvie assured her conscience. She truly hadn't minded giving her sister the needed financial assistance. It was the time-and-effort commitment she had made, admittedly of her own free will, that bothered her. Juliette had never been good with commitments of any kind, and Sylvie had done more than her fair share of assuming the responsibility. Yet, despite that knowledge, she had agreed not only to help finance this latest venture, but volunteered to spend six months getting it organized.

To be fair, she had been looking for an excuse to get away from the office, anyway. The insurance-investigation business had lost its appeal to Sylvie. Max's suggestion that her heart needed space for adjustment wasn't accurate, but Sylvie knew that something had occurred to strip the challenge from her work. She didn't know why she was surprised. It was a familiar pattern in her life. The restlessness that led her into one career or area of interest eventually always led her into another. So, here she was in Eureka Springs, next door to a self-appointed Lothario and listening to Juliette's endless stream of conversation. Why hadn't her yen for new surroundings taken her to Waikiki or the south of France?

Because no matter how she tried, she just couldn't say no to Juliette. It was not, Sylvie realized, a problem singular to her; everyone had trouble when it came to refusing Juliette. From the moment of her birth on a perfect spring morning, Juliette had moved through life blithely unaware that the world hadn't been created solely for her delight. She wasn't spoiled—Sylvie had seen personally to that—she was simply optimistic that no matter what happened, somehow, some way, everything would turn out right. And, inexplicably, everything always did. The dress shop would be no different.

". . . and upstairs there's a little alcove that will be perfect. . . ."

The words were an enthusiastic accompaniment to her thoughts, and Sylvie let her lips curve with affection. Once someone had asked her if she was jealous of her sister's Shirley Temple cuteness and Pollyanna charm, but Sylvie had been amazed at the question. Perhaps it was because she'd been older, an awkward but mature seven, when Juliette was born, that Sylvie had bypassed the usual feelings of sibling rivalry. Or perhaps it was because their mother had died when they were very young that the girls had formed a closer bond than most sisters. Or perhaps, Sylvie thought now, she had long ago simply accepted her role as guardian angel to Juliette's free spirit.

There had been times—there still were occasions even now—when she resented the mere fact of not being an only child, but those times were infrequent and inconsequential. There had been very little conflict of interest over the years. Probably because they had vastly different opinions on everything from studying to fad diets. And their goals had always been poles apart. Sylvie was achievement oriented. She could list dozens of accomplishments and skills she had mastered. Juliette, on the other hand, expended her energies only on enjoying all that life offered. And life, in apparent appreciation, rewarded her with love. Everyone loved Juliette. Despite the frustrations Sylvie was no exception.

". . . and Mr. Erikson. He's the man who owned the house and did most of the renovation. But he got sick, you know, and couldn't complete the work . . . and then he died. But luckily he signed the papers first. Well, not luckily for him, of course, but it is lucky I decided to buy the house before . . ."

With a nod of unnecessary encouragement Sylvie continued to listen to a story she had heard several times during the past few months through the miracle of modern telephone service. She wondered if Max McConnell loved Juliette. He certainly hadn't acted as if he were too entranced. But then, what did she really know about him?

Sylvie pressed her back against the kitchen counter and decided she knew more than enough to justify a niggling worry. With a tiny frown she waited for Juliette to break for breath. "Are you serious about Max, Julie?"

"Serious?" Her forehead puckered in confusion as Juliette made an obvious effort to assimilate the change of conversational topic. "In what way?"

"How many ways are there?"

"Well, there's emotionally serious and there's physically serious and then there's . . ." Twin dimples made a mischievous interruption. "But when it comes to Max, I don't think we need to go any further, do you?"

Sylvie felt another sigh threatening to escape her throat. "Are you or are you not in love with the man?"

"Max? Oh, I wouldn't say that I'm in love with him . . . exactly."

"Well, what, exactly, would you say? If you're not emotionally serious about him, then—God, Juliette, surely you're not sleeping with him?"

"Only in my most secret fantasies." Juliette sighed

dramatically, even as her mouth formed an impish smile. "You've only been in town a couple of hours and already you've seen more of him than I usually do."

"That certainly isn't the impression you gave me over the telephone."

"I know, but I didn't want you to think life in Eureka Springs was dull."

Sylvie slid her glasses to the end of her nose and observed her sister with a slightly unfocused gaze. She was quickly remembering how exasperating Juliette could be. "Let's go see our investment, shall we?"

"Does that mean you're not going to tell me how he looked without his clothes?"

"I can't tell you something I don't know." She pushed the tortoiseshell frames back into place and began to fold the empty grocery sacks. "After all, he was decently covered."

Juliette released an appealing giggle. "Decently covered? Oh, come on, Sylvie Anne, why not admit that you were *indecently* impressed?"

At that point Sylvie knew there was no future in stating her very definite opinion. Juliette had always been able to argue common logic down to a frazzled reason. "All right," Sylvie conceded in exchange for peace. "Your next-door neighbor is an attractive man."

"And?"

"And nothing. He isn't my type."

"How do you know? You just met him."

"I just *know*, Juliette. Besides, I thought he was your latest romance."

With a tiny shrug Juliette slid her foot back inside

her shoe. "Actually, he hasn't seemed all that interested in me. Max has been very nice and we've gone to dinner a few times, but . . ."

As Juliette rose, Sylvie held out the sacks she'd folded and told herself she wouldn't ask because she didn't want to know. But the question came of its own volition, with only minimal assistance from her. "But what?"

"Oh, I don't know." Juliette took the sacks and dropped them into the trash. "There's something . . . Max and I don't seem to be on the same level of communication at times."

Which Sylvie could easily understand. At times it was impossible to know what level of communication Juliette was on. "I can't believe he doesn't have a few secret fantasies himself. I'm sure he'll come around," she said in reassurance, although it was against her better judgment. "I've never before seen a man who didn't come around with you."

Juliette wrinkled her nose in disagreement. "I don't think so. Max just doesn't have a . . . a special smile for me." She offered the information in a cheerful voice. "And don't ask me to explain, because I can't. I just know. So if you're interested in Max, feel free."

"You're too generous, Juliette. But I'm sure we'll all be happier if you and I stay on our side of the property line and Max stays on his."

"I can't promise that." The dimples made a fleeting reappearance. "What will we do when we run out of eggs or coffee or something? Max is the only neighbor I can borrow from."

Sylvie slid her hands into the side pockets of her dress and took a purposeful step toward the door.

"From now on we'll make sure we don't run out of anything."

"Easy for you to say, Sylvie Anne. Personally, I intend to keep borrowing from Max until *I* get to see him in a towel."

"Believe me, it wasn't that great a sight." Retrieving her purse from the credenza in the front hall, Sylvie opened the door and found herself face to face with the rebuttal of her lie. Max stood there, his hand poised to knock, his mouth slanting slowly into a smile. He was still wearing the plaid flannel shirt and faded jeans, but he had shaved the morning shadow from his jaw. Her heart unaccountably skipped a beat, and then another, before her gaze fell to his feet. At least, she thought, he had put on a pair of shoes. Although she hesitated to classify the well-worn, stale-looking sneakers as shoes.

"Hello," he said. "You're leaving?"

"Yes," she stated flatly, banning from her mind the recognition that he was indeed physically attractive. This was hardly the appropriate time for noticing that.

"Hi, Max," Juliette called from a few steps behind Sylvie. "Need to borrow something?"

"Just the pleasure of your company." His blue eyes tossed a casual challenge to Sylvie. "And your sister's, of course."

Of course. Sylvie channeled her renewed irritation into a calm, almost regretful, smile. "Well, as I said," she began, "we're leaving."

"What did you have in mind, Max?" Juliette moved to share the doorway with Sylvie. "We're open to all offers."

"I thought we might have dinner tonight. Since

this is Sylvie Anne's first day in town, we ought to have a bit of a celebration."

Sylvie raised her eyebrows. "We? That's a rather vague pronoun, Max."

"Oh, I think it's pretty clear. We, as in the three of us, are going to have dinner together."

"That's very thoughtful, but—"

"What time should we be ready?"

"Juliette!" Sylvie tightened the corners of her smile and shot her sister a warning look. "Remember? We, as in just the two of us, planned to have a nice, quiet evening and catch up on everything?"

Juliette's response was a melodic laugh. "Are you kidding? We've got six months of quiet evenings and TV dinners ahead of us. How often are we going to get an invitation like this?" Her eager grin was exclusively for Max.

What could she say to that? Sylvie didn't dare mention that she had no intention of eating frozen dinners at any time during the next six months. If Max found out she could cook, he'd probably invite himself to share the pleasure of their company for the next one hundred and eighty days. She sighed in momentary defeat and silently started planning an evening headache. "Thank you, Max. What time should we be ready?"

The curve of his lips was exclusively for her, and she returned it with a less-than-encouraging frown.

"Seven, give or take an hour. I'd be more definite, Sylvie Anne, but I've been out with your sister before."

"That isn't nice, Max," Juliette said easily. "But I'll forgive you this one time. We're on our way to Hannah Lee House. Why don't you come along?"

Sylvie bit her tongue to keep from voicing her objection. She didn't want to sound petty, even though she felt she had every reason to feel that way.

"Another time, Julie." Max took a step back. "There are some things I have to do at my store this afternoon. You can tell me all about your restored bargain again when I see you tonight." In one smooth glance he shared his teasing grin with Sylvie and made her wish for the warm sunshine of Waikiki Beach. "And you can tell me what you think, Sylvie Anne."

"With great pleasure," she replied, her mind already composing a few choice phrases. "I'll look forward to it."

"What should we wear, Max?" Juliette moved past Sylvie and stepped outside. "Sylvie worries about things like that, you know."

"Does she?" His tone was gently curious as his gaze swept over Sylvie with unnecessary attention to detail. She closed her eyes and divided her annoyance equally between the two people standing in front of her. Then she opened her eyes, touched the rim of her glasses, and silently mimicked the answer she knew was coming.

"Wear something casual," he said, and she smiled. Casual, she thought, just about summed Max McConnell up.

"I can hardly wait." Juliette reached behind her for the doorknob, urging Sylvie out of the house ahead of the closing door. "I have a new outfit that—"

"Surprise us, Julie. All right?" With a last lingering smile Max turned and began walking across the narrow yard between the houses.

Sylvie watched him and thought he ought to swagger a little to justify her opinion of him. But he didn't. His stride was even and controlled and had an affect on her that couldn't be termed casual. She could think of several terms that were applicable, but *casual* was definitely not one of them.

"He's interested, Sylvie."

Juliette sounded unusually confident and Sylvie turned in surprise. "Of course he is, Juliette. I told you he'd come around."

"Oh, Sylvie Anne, sometimes I think you're a babe in the woods when it comes to men. Max is interested in *you*, not me."

Sylvie considered the idea while she adjusted her glasses, but the only conclusion she reached was that the idea wasn't worth considering. "Well, if he's hoping to be included in *my* fantasies, he's going to be disappointed."

Juliette didn't smile. "I don't know how I could have raised you to have such a bad attitude toward men. Honestly, Sylvie, if I didn't know you better, I'd say you were scared of getting involved."

"There's no need to get worked up about it. I told you that Max just isn't my type." Sylvie tucked her handbag in the crook of her arm and started toward the car.

"He isn't safe, you mean."

Stopping abruptly, Sylvie released an intentional and audible sigh of annoyance. "I meant, and I mean, that he isn't my type."

Juliette wisely walked to the other side of the car before voicing another opinion. "You shouldn't tempt fate with that kind of remark. After all, you haven't seen Max in his plaid sport coat yet." Blithely ignoring Sylvie's cool look, Juliette observed her questioningly. "What are you doing? No one drives in downtown Eureka Springs if they can help it. And we can. Come on, we're walking."

Sylvie had a sudden longing to see the familiar, busy, and cultured efficiency of Boston, where the men wore pinstripe suits and where she could afford to talk to Juliette not more than once a month. With a last, lingering sigh and a certain amount of good grace, she fell into step with her sister.

CHAPTER THREE

Sylvie spent the better part of the afternoon wandering through the hallways, doorways, and alcoves of Hannah Lee House. Juliette spent the same amount of time talking, pointing out work already completed and areas still needing attention. Sylvie listened attentively, or pretended to do so, as she formed her own judgments about suitable decor and arrangement of rooms. The house was lovely, an old Victorian with quaint charm. By the time she had heard—for at least the seventeenth time—the plans for finishing the renovation work begun by the late Mr. Erikson, Sylvie's attitude was on the upswing.

She had never been involved in the clothing business, but that didn't worry her. If Juliette was blessed with luck when it came to affairs of the heart, Sylvie knew *she* was blessed with an aptitude for success. The dress shop, featuring recycled clothing from past decades, would open in March when the tourist season began, and it would be a successful venture. Sylvie didn't doubt it for a moment, but she was realistic enough not to underestimate the amount of work that would be required during the coming months.

As she watched Juliette roam dreamily from room

to room, touching the walls, then the woodwork, then the walls again, Sylvie resolved once more not to carry more than her fair share of the responsibility this time. Juliette was fond of imagining the finished product, but she tended to ignore the production line. And she was very good at leaving the details to someone else.

"It's wonderful, isn't it, Syl?"

The sparkle in Juliette's eyes, the excitement in her voice, rattled the windows of Sylvie's doubts, chastening her for even thinking of past mistakes and negative possibilities.

"It's wonderful, Juliette." From years of conditioning she gave the reassurance she knew her sister needed. "I think you're going to have a thriving business. It will take a lot of work, but from what I could see of the town, the type of clothing store you have in mind should fit right in."

"I got the idea of recyling clothes from this woman I met in Fayetteville. You should see her shop, Sylvie." Juliette circled the front room, smiling as if she were taking a curtain call. "But I told you about that, didn't I?"

"Yes, you did."

Trailing her fingertips over the wall covering, Juliette assumed the graceful movements of a ballerina. It reminded Sylvie of the hours *she* had spent in learning to dance. Juliette's interest in ballet had consisted mainly of choosing the most flattering color for her costumes.

Sylvie caught a strand of hair and anchored it behind her ear as she turned to look at the street through the front window. "Now that I've seen the most important site in Arkansas, I think I should at least take a look at the rest of the town. You've been telling me for months that Eureka Springs is quite a place, but on the way here, you walked so fast I didn't have a chance to see much of it."

"*I* walked so fast? My God, Sylvie, I thought you were in training for a marathon or something."

"Just trying to keep pace with your patter."

"Funny, I thought you might be in a hurry to put as much distance as possible between us and Max."

"Us?" Sylvie arched her brows in skeptical question. "Don't you think that would be wasted effort, considering how eager you were to accept his dinner invitation?"

"How could I turn down a celebration in *your* honor, Sylvie Anne?" Juliette's expression was her own unique blend of devilry and innocence. "I was only thinking of you . . . and how much you'd hate to have to cook tonight."

"Well, you can think of me when you explain to Max why I won't be joining the two of you for dinner."

Juliette shrugged with an artful indifference. "Afraid of the competition?" she asked. "Even after I told you Max isn't interested in me?"

"Is that supposed to give me a head start in the race for his attention?" Sylvie tucked her purse into place with a snap of her elbow. "Thanks, but I'd rather sight-see now and have a headache later."

"Well, no one deserves a headache more. Stay home if you want, Sylvie Anne. I must say, though, that sulking doesn't suit you."

Ignoring the blatant attempt to shame her into changing her mind, Sylvie walked to the door and waited, perfectly comfortable with her decision. Juliette drew a deep, very audible breath and made one last survey of her domain. "I suppose it wouldn't hurt to do a bit of sight-seeing. We've got plenty of time before our—excuse me—*my* date with Max." She walked to the door and waited for Sylvie to precede her outside. Then she closed the door, patted the stained-glass inset, and turned the key in the lock. "It's just as well you've decided not to come with us tonight, Sylvie. It would probably be embarrassing for you to sit there while I tell Max how you used to worry about being so skinny and underdeveloped"— her pause was slight and sly—"how you *still* worry. . . ."

Sylvie smiled with benign frustration. "You were born too late to blackmail me, my little sister. I, on the other hand, know things about you that Max Mc-Connell would give his left tennis shoe to know. But I really don't think he can do without the shoe, so let's forget—"

"Sylvie, Max doesn't want to know about *me*. He's not, n-o-t, interested. Besides, I've been thinking about this all afternoon. I'm really not interested in him either."

"Well, let me congratulate you on your good judgment." Sylvie started to walk in the direction of the shop next door, only to stop when she realized Juliette wasn't beside her. Turning back, she felt a definite twinge of conscience. Juliette had sucked in her lower lip, a gesture Sylvie knew well. It meant she felt strongly about the subject, whatever the subject of the moment might be, and she was preparing to defend her position.

"I don't know when you developed that chip on your shoulder, Sylvie Anne Smith, but I don't like it one bit. Max is one of the nicest, most attractive, most dependable, most . . ." She gave her blond curls a boisterous toss. "With that kind of attitude, you'll be lucky if his interest in you lasts through dinner."

Sylvie realized she'd lost count of the number of sighs that had escaped her in the past few hours. But whatever the total had been, it was now one more. "Juliette, Max is not interested in me. You're imagining something that doesn't exist."

"My imagination has never been that good." Juliette caught up to Sylvie and set a leisurely pace as they walked along the sidewalk. "And even if it were, even if I imagined that odd look in his eyes, you ought to make sure he *gets* interested. How often does a man like Max come along?"

The question seemed so melodramatic, so Victorian, that Sylvie had to laugh. "So seldom, Juliette, it scares me to think of it. And you know, with a little bit of luck, I might have missed the experience altogether." With a teasing smile Sylvie turned her attention to the window of a confectioner's store.

"God will get you for that, Sylvie. Someday, you'll get what's coming." The dire promise faded away as Juliette sniffed the air like a connoisseur of fine scents and stepped forward to enter the shop. "Come on, I want to introduce you to some truly wicked fudge."

Max was forgotten for the time being, and as Sylvie followed her sister and the aroma of chocolate into the store, she resolved to buy enough candy to keep him overshadowed in Juliette's one-track mind.

During the next hour Juliette nibbled her way through three different assortments of sweets and refrained from mentioning Max at all. Sylvie wasn't even tempted to sample the candy, but twice she came within a breath of asking a question about Max. It was an unsettling sensation to realize that there were things she wanted to know about him. And it was even more unsettling to realize she'd stated such a strong opinion that it would be impossible to bring up his name without putting Juliette right back on the track of a conversation that was better left derailed.

The rest of the afternoon passed in an enjoyable discovery of the shops and craftsmen that made the town a popular tourist spot, but Sylvie's feeling of disquiet lingered. She had a distinct sense of looking for something that eluded her. When Juliette stopped in front of a toy-filled window shortly before four o'clock, Sylvie knew what she'd been looking for.

The Attic was a small shop, gaily painted in bright, splashy colors. Through the glass panes Sylvie could see a room full of whimsy, a fantasy land of toys that she shrewdly guessed would tempt adults as much as, if not more than, children. So this, she thought, was the business side of Max McConnell.

"Ah, I knew if you chose the stops on our sightseeing tour, we'd get to Max's shop eventually," Juliette said sweetly. "Now that we're here, we may as well go inside. That way you can explain to him in person why you're too chicken to go out with him tonight."

In reply Sylvie leaned closer to the window, cupping her hands around the tortoiseshell frames at her temples to press against the glass and block the sun's glare. Her effort was rewarded with an enchanting display of dolls and dollhouses, wooden trucks and trains, a miniature carousel and a full-size carousel horse. It had been years, Sylvie thought, since she had been anywhere near a toy store. But the tug of enchantment was still strong. Her fingers chafed with the desire to touch and her mouth curved with happy childhood memories.

She looked up and found herself gazing into two incredibly blue eyes. As Max watched her, a sudden, warm pleasure whispered through her senses. Then it was gone. As if he knew exactly what she was experiencing, from sensation to practical explanation, Max smiled confidently and motioned her to join him. Juliette was already through the doorway when Sylvie straightened and debated the possibility of waiting outside. But she dismissed the idea as ridiculous, and with a quick adjustment of her glasses she entered the toy store.

The interior was just as gingerbread bright as the exterior, and the carousel horse drew Sylvie forward with all the lure of a calliope. Juliette had apparently seen it all before, and she walked to the counter where Max stood, explaining with each step how Sylvie had wanted to see where he worked. Sylvie tried to ignore the imaginative story of her interest in Max and his workshop and reached out to touch the smooth, painted surface of the carved horse.

"Be careful." Max came around the side of the counter as Sylvie glanced at him in surprise, her fingers hesitating an inch away from the horse's wooden nose. "He's not an ordinary wooden horse. He's magical."

Sylvie frowned and shook her head. Nonsense. She was surrounded by nonsense. First Juliette and now Max. In outright defiance she placed her hand on the horse. "What kind of tricks does he do?"

Max's lips slanted with wry amusement. "No tricks, just magic. He's a wishing horse."

What a line, Sylvie thought, even from a man who owned a toy shop. "Well, what is he wishing for?"

"Don't be ridiculous, Sylvie," Juliette advised from her perch on the counter top. *"You're* supposed to make the wish."

Which was ridiculous, but Sylvie realized she was the only one who seemed to recognize that. She lifted a resigned expression to Max. "Do I have to say 'please' and 'thank you'?" she asked dryly.

"You don't have to say a thing, Sylvie Anne. All you have to do"—Max's gaze dropped to her fingers which were moving idly over the wood—"is rub his nose three times and make a wish."

Sylvie couldn't keep from laughing, although her fingers stilled of their own accord. "This is amazing. Did he come with complete instructions or are you just a clever salesman?"

"I like to think I'm pretty clever. And, since I made McKeever, here"—he gave the horse an affectionate pat—"I guess I can take credit for the instructions too."

Sylvie gave a sharp, appraising scrutiny to the wood beneath her hand. It was a beautiful replica, a carefully detailed carving, and she could hardly believe Max had created it. "You made this?" Her voice reflected her doubt, and the silence that followed was tinged with discomfort until Juliette saved the moment with a bubbly laugh.

"Of course he made it, Sylvie Anne. Max makes all the toys in his shop."

Her appraising look, of its own accord, swung to Max. She realized her reaction was not flattering and that she ought to offer some form of apology, but she didn't know how to do that without making the situation worse. Besides, after the nonsense he'd dished out, Max deserved a bit of skepticism.

"You made all of these?" she asked, her gaze surveying the room, accepting his skill as a woodcarver, but balking at some of the other creations.

"I take some things on consignment from other people. That dollhouse, for example." He pointed to a three-story house with yellow wood shingles. "A philosophy professor at the university in Little Rock made it. He brings two or three dollhouses to me every year, and so far they've all sold."

"Except that one." Juliette leaned forward, her elbows on her knees, chin propped in her hands. "Max is saving it for his little girl."

For no apparent reason Sylvie's stomach dropped. *His little girl?* She looked to him for confirmation, but he was looking at her sister with an expression of exasperated amusement.

"Can you repeat every word that has ever been said to you, Julie?"

"Word for word, usually," she agreed, with a teasing display of her dimples. "Just ask Sylvie Anne."

Max's blue eyes met Sylvie's green ones and the tension snapped inside her. She lifted her chin and straightened her glasses. "She doesn't repeat everything," Sylvie said. "As amazing as it might seem, Juliette neglected to tell me about your daughter."

Laughter rumbled deep in his throat. "Not so amazing considering that I don't have one. I happened to mention to Julie once that *if* I should ever have a child, I'd probably go bankrupt. I'd want to give him or her everything in the store. And that dollhouse would be the first thing to be wrapped in a pink or blue ribbon."

"That wouldn't be good for business."

His smile held steady, but only with a definite effort. "Maybe not, but what a boring world it would be if we only did what was good for us."

"I suppose that's a comfortable theory, considering that it will never be put to the test." Sylvie turned to the assortment of dolls that lined the shelves. In a matter of steps she had moved away from Max and his wishing horse and into another section of the store. A safer and saner section, she hoped.

But Sylvie realized her mistake with her first careful look at the shelves. Here, too, was magic. The leftover magic of childhood memories and her own past delight in a Christmas doll. From the soft-sculpture, fuzzy-haired ragamuffin to the delicate porcelain face and hands of Cinderella, each doll was exquisite. Sylvie moved closer, her fingers reaching impulsively to touch the satin gown of one doll, the fur muff of another.

Her gaze fell to a baby in a quilted basket. Its porcelain mouth formed a pout and its tiny hands were poised in a lifelike position. The christening gown was made of a gauzy white fabric, embroidered with lace and ribbon. The bonnet was layers of ruching with a narrow ribbon tie. Sylvie didn't know a great deal about dolls, but she knew these were exceptionally detailed and beautiful.

"I think she wants you to hold her," Max said, and Sylvie's hand fell to her side as he reached past her to lift the baby from the basket.

"I think you're insane," she muttered. She would have turned away, but his smile held her still as he placed the doll in her arms. It was absurd, she knew, but the doll felt oddly real nestled in the cradle of her arms. She looked into the sleeping face, touched the tiny fingers and the dimpled chin, and felt the stirring of new emotions as she lifted her gaze to Max. As he looked down at her, the expression in his eyes seemed somehow reassuring, almost tender. He was standing close . . . so very close. . . .

Sylvie practically shoved the doll at him. "I suppose you made her—it too?"

Max took the doll and placed it in the basket again. With the skill of an artist he draped the christening gown in delicate folds and Sylvie wondered at his gentleness.

"Yes, as a matter of fact, I did." He straightened, his eyes daring Sylvie to comment. "I made all of the dolls except that one." He pointed out the cloth ragamuffin. "I prefer working with porcelain."

Sylvie made one last effort to conceal her amazement and growing respect, but knew she didn't succeed. "You made—" She swallowed the inexplicable need to repeat his statement. "The clothing," she said instead. "Do you make that too?"

"I have some help with that. My hands are too big to manage some of the detail work, so I concentrate on designing the doll and let my assistant do the sewing."

"Where is Miriam today?" Juliette asked as she jumped down from the counter to include herself in the conversation. "She's usually here on Saturdays."

"She left yesterday to visit her granddaughter in Cincinnati. I threatened her wih early retirement, but she wasn't impressed. I'm on my own this week."

"You don't have to be. Sylvie and I will be glad to help if we can. Won't we, Syl?"

"We have plenty to do already, Juliette." Sylvie protested mildly. "You have your own business to attend to, remember?"

Juliette frowned her disenchantment with that idea. "Of course I remember. But we can spare a few hours to help Max." She turned to Max. "I can't sew a button on, but Sylvie is quite a seamstress. She makes all her own clothes, you know."

Max turned to Sylvie, unable to resist imitating her earlier expression of disbelief. "You made that outfit?" He gave free rein to the incredulous tone in his voice and was rewarded by the flash of irritation in her green eyes. "I'm impressed, Sylvie. If you're ever in need of a job, just let me know."

"Thanks, but I think I'm a bit too rational to work here." She toyed with the slim leather strap of her shoulder bag as she let her gaze wander around the room. "Besides," she continued, bringing her attention back to the teasing challenge in his eyes, "I didn't make this dress. It's been years since I did any sewing. You can't always believe what Juliette says."

"Can I believe what you say, Sylvie?"

"Oh, absolutely." She gave her most convincing smile, despite Juliette's annoying giggle.

It was not a genuine smile. Max realized that and was beginning to think he'd imagined the intriguing possibility of a warm, responsive woman beneath her cool sophistication. But still, there had been an oddly vulnerable expression in her eyes when she held the doll in her arms. That had surprised him. Not as much as he apparently had surprised her, though. Sylvie had done a fair job of flattening his ego this afternoon. Maybe he was crazy not to plead a headache and cancel tonight's dinner. But, what the hell, he didn't have any other plans and Sylvie was amusing.

"I guess that means you'll be ready at seven, then."

"Of course it does," Juliette answered before Sylvie had a chance to speak. "We're going home right now to start getting ready. It takes me a while, you know. And, although Sylvie would never admit it, she takes her own sweet time too." Juliette offered a saucy grin. "It's all the aspirin she takes."

Max nodded his understanding. "Do you have trouble with headaches, Sylvie Anne?"

"Ever since I was seven years old." Sylvie's hands went to either side of the tortoiseshell frames of her glasses. "I think it's time we were going, Julie." She warned her sister with a look and moved to the door.

"Why don't you walk home with us, Max?" Juliette asked as she slowly followed Sylvie's direction.

"Juliette," Sylvie protested before Max had a chance to do so, "he can't just close the store whenever he feels like it."

"Of course he can. Everyone else does. That's one of the nice things about Eureka Springs. If you don't want to work, you just close up shop and go home. Isn't that right, Max?"

Sylvie shook her head at the idea. "It isn't a good way to do business. I'm sure Max is aware of that."

He was trapped between two opposing points of view and Max decided he'd be damned if he'd cater to either one of them. "Oh, I don't know. It seems like a good method to me," he answered Sylvie. "But I can't leave just yet," he answered Juliette. "I'll see you both tonight."

He stepped forward to open the door, but whatever else he might have added was lost as two elderly women with large purses and empty shopping bags approached the entrance. Max calmly flipped the OPEN sign to CLOSED. "I'm sorry," he said with a sincerely regretful and totally disarming smile. "We're closed for the day. Try us another time."

The potential customers grumbled good-naturedly as they turned away, and Sylvie stared after them in disbelief. She would have turned the stare to Max if he hadn't ushered her out the door and onto the sidewalk beside Juliette.

"Tonight," he repeated before closing the door with a definitive click.

Sylvie's first impulse was to follow the two women and explain that The Attic would be open the next day and that they should certainly return then. But of course she couldn't do that, mainly because she had no idea if The Attic *would* be open the next day. Apparently Max was as casual about business hours as he was about—

"Are you coming with me?"

The sound of impatience broke into her thoughts and Sylvie looked up to see that Juliette was already some distance away. With a last quizzical glance at the toy shop door she joined her sister. "He's really something. Closing shop in the middle of the afternoon with customers right there in front of him."

Juliette shrugged, demonstrating her lack of concern. "It's his store, you know, and his prerogative. He can do whatever he wants."

"But it's bad for business, Juliette. Prerogative or no, turning away customers is not a good idea. I hope you realize the importance of regular store hours."

"Oh, I do." Juliette waved gaily to someone across the street. "And I wouldn't dream of closing early— at least not while you're here to hold my nose to the grindstone."

That hurt, and Sylvie didn't intend to let it pass. She came to an abrupt halt in the center of the sidewalk. "In that case I'll leave you to dig your own ditches."

Juliette stopped, her china-blue eyes brimming with apology. "You know I didn't mean anything by it, Sylvie Anne. I want you to stay. I need your help. It's just that sometimes . . . well, you don't seem to understand that there's more than one way to do things."

Sylvie acknowledged the possible truth of that, but she still held to her opinion that success didn't come without a certain amount of effort and a great deal of self-discipline.

"All right, Julie, I'll try to be more open minded if you'll give me the benefit of the doubt when it comes to how to succeed in business. But you have to promise you won't take Max as your example."

"I promise not to take him as my anything. He wouldn't let me anyway. He's all yours, Sylvie dear."

If she had learned anything over the years, Sylvie had learned when it was futile to argue with her sister. Breathing a sigh of frustration, she began walking again and Juliette matched her steps. It was almost a full minute before she became aware of Juliette's wide grin and another thirty seconds before she asked the inevitable question. "What are you so happy about?"

"I'm just glad you're here, Sylvie Anne. You know," Juliette said thoughtfully, "I believe I've done you a tremendous favor in asking you to help me start this business."

"Should I thank you now or later?" Sylvie asked dryly.

Juliette simply responded with a coyly omniscient smile. "Oh, you can wait until tonight. After we've had dinner with Max. That will be soon enough to express your undying gratitude."

"I'm not going to dinner tonight."

"Of course you are. You don't have anything else to do, and besides . . ." Juliette let the sentence slide as she paused in front of a window display. "What do you think of that blue sweater, Syl?" Tilting her head to the side, Juliette shook her head and answered her own question. "No, you're right. The shade is too pale for me."

"You should listen to me more often, Juliette." Sylvie kept walking, hoping they weren't too far from the house and a hot, relaxing, and blessedly quiet bath.

"Besides," Juliette picked up her first train of thought as if there hadn't been a break. "Going with Max and me tonight is the only way you can prove that you're really not a coward. You have an image to uphold, Sylvie. You're my older sister and I look up to you."

Aspirin, Sylvie thought. She was definitely going to need some aspirin.

CHAPTER FOUR

It was six-fifteen before Sylvie finally agreed to forego excuses and join her sister and Max for dinner. In exchange Juliette promised never again to accept an invitation on Sylvie's behalf. She also promised, more reluctantly and under penalty of losing her new angora sweater, that on their return home there would be no discussion of, no comment on, and absolutely no recap of the evening. Sylvie bore up well to Juliette's rejoinder that no self-respecting redhead would wear the sweater's particular shade of pink anyway, and silently hoped it wouldn't have to be put to the test.

By five past seven, Sylvie was ready, although not enthusiastic, for the evening ahead. Juliette, who was never short on enthusiasm, wasn't ready until seven-forty, just in time to breeze past Sylvie's impatiently tapping foot and open the door to Max's knock.

"Perfect timing, Max," Juliette announced in dimpled welcome. "We've been counting the seconds."

"Have you?" Max looked directly at Sylvie with a smile of definite intentions.

"Oh, yes. All twenty-four hundred of them," Sylvie replied with a smile designed to cool those same intentions. "And don't bother to check my multiplication. No matter how you try, it won't add up to seven o'clock."

His laughter was slow and soft. "Anticipation does lend a certain ambience to an evening, doesn't it?"

"So does hunger." Sylvie walked past him to the doorway in the hope that positive action might get the evening under way. "Shall we go?"

"Oops! I forgot to get my . . ." Juliette ran toward the bedroom in search of something and Max stepped close to Sylvie.

"Hello, Sylvie Anne. You look very nice tonight. Blue is very becoming to you."

Becoming? She hadn't heard that vague expression in years and certainly never in connection with this particular dress. Still, his voice was sincere, and Sylvie felt her pulse quicken.

"Thank you," she said as she ran a practiced eye over the brown herringbone jacket he'd slung carelessly across his arm, the white short-sleeve shirt he wore, and the indigo-blue of his jeans. It was a casual outfit, worn for comfort rather than style, although Sylvie had to admit the style suited Max well. Quite well. And at least he wasn't wearing plaid. "You look very nice too."

"It's my cologne, Attention Getter. Every time I wear it, a beautiful woman pays me a compliment."

Sylvie placed an index finger on either side of her glasses and readjusted her focus. This time she turned her gaze to his face and noted the clean-cut angle of his jaw, the laughter lines at the corners of his mouth and eyes, the dark arch of his brows, and the crisp hint of curl in his hair. And every feature communicated his underlying amusement. Sylvie just couldn't decide if he was amused by her or by life in general. "Well, in that case, you certainly should purchase cologne in quantity," she replied with a laugh.

He chuckled softly and then bent toward her. Sylvie would have stepped away, but the door frame was at her back and she didn't want to rush out onto the porch as if she were afraid of him. Which she wasn't, of course, but—what was he *doing?*

His nose almost touched her shoulder and in that one split second of closeness a dozen different sensations sashayed through her body. He did smell nice, she realized. He had a good, clean, natural scent like wind and water and sunlight. And his hair did curl, just a little, at his neckline. For some completely incomprehensible reason she wondered if her hands were big enough to measure the width of his chest. Ridiculous thought. Her hands were big enough to give his chest a hearty shove, and that was all that counted.

But then he was moving back, his eyes catching hers for a moment that held no trace of laughter. And then, as if it had never been, the moment vanished. His expression lightened and his lips formed a teasing frown of concentration. "I'm not sure I recognize the fragrance you're wearing, Sylvie. Is it Passé or Thriller?"

"It's called No Nonsense." She lifted her chin and smiled sweetly. "Would you like me to spell it out for you?"

"Wait until it's closer to Christmas. I might forget between now and then and get you the wrong bottle of perfume."

"Max McConnell," Juliette said as she joined them in the entryway. "Don't you dare let Sylvie talk you into buying perfume for her. She won't wear it. She says there's no reason to encourage a man to think—"

"I think we ought to leave now." Sylvie squelched the rest of Juliette's comment with a pointed look. "Before I decide to change into something pink."

Max placed a hand on the door and Sylvie walked past him, followed closely by Juliette.

"You're not getting my sweater, Sylvie. Besides, that bet doesn't start until we get home tonight, and I told you already that pink won't be a good color for you. Don't you agree?" She turned the question to Max, who was closing the door. "Oh, wait, Max. I forgot"—the door clicked shut—"my key."

It was not a good beginning for a celebration.

". . . but Sylvie told him she wasn't about to . . ."

Sylvie took a long, slow drink of iced tea and wondered if anyone in the restaurant would notice if she yawned. Silly idea. There was hardly anyone in the restaurant, other than herself, Max, and Juliette. An elderly couple sat in the far corner, and on the other side of the room a man sat alone eating his dinner. Altogether that made six customers, and Sylvie had counted two different people who apparently took turns at the cash register, waiting for any or all of the six to pay their bill.

". . . and it was a touch-and-go thing, until Sylvie got home. But then . . ."

Sylvie stifled the yawn and regarded Max with a mixture of grudging respect and growing irritation. By rights he should be yawning. He deserved to be bored, but it was his fault that Juliette kept talking . . . and talking. There was no doubt in Sylvie's mind that Max was encouraging her sister's embarrassing recital of long-dead adventures—or misadventures, depending on one's point of view. Setting her glass on the table, Sylvie was glad, at least, that the food hadn't matched the dinner conversation.

The restaurant was neat and cozy, if not busy. But then, most people ate dinner at an earlier hour. With a glance at her watch Sylvie reached for her glass again.

". . . and then, my date—I've forgotten his name, but he was the shortest player on the basketball team. At least, he was short then, he might be taller now. Well, my date had brought a bottle of vodka—God knows where he got it—and since Sylvie was the chaperone that night she . . ."

Juliette was on a roll, it seemed, and Max was listening attentively to every word, although his eyes were often on Sylvie. He'd been flirting with her that way all evening. It was a subtle and, for the most part, silent courtship, but Sylvie recognized his attempts to coax her smile, to capture her gaze with his own, to entice her to play the game. She just couldn't seem to get across the message that he was wasting his time.

With arms crossed over his chest and his shoulders resting against the chairback, his posture was one of easy confidence. Or maybe *lazy* would be a more appropriate adjective. Even *insolent* would work, although Sylvie admitted that her assessment was not objective.

That bothered her, because she was always objective when it came to men. Even when she was strongly attracted to a man, she was careful to keep her perspective. But with Max she hadn't been able to get a grip on what that perspective should be. And that was an unfamiliar feeling and a very unsettling realization, one she didn't want to experience often.

She absently traced a rivulet down the side of her water glass, analyzing the reason for Max's unmistakable interest in her and her lack of indifference about it. But the logic, if there was any logic involved, eluded her and faded into the sunny vivaciousness of Juliette's voice.

". . . and since Sylvie Anne had taken a first-aid class, there was no reason to panic. . . ."

Juliette's voice always amazed Max and invariably left him a little breathless. It wasn't her wide variation of inflections or even her pleasant soprano tone, it was the sheer unbroken rhythm she maintained that fascinated him. He always felt as if he should take a deep breath whenever Julie opened her mouth to speak.

Of course, most of her monologue this evening had been at his instigation. Every time she paused or turned an inquisitive look to her sister, he posed another question, urging her to continue. It wasn't the gentlemanly thing to do, he knew, but he *was* interested and he wanted to see just how long Sylvie Anne could sustain her composed, polite expression. Indefinitely, it seemed, although he thought she was beginning to show signs of stress.

Her finger was drawing a steady, repetitive pattern on the sweaty side of her glass and Max felt sure that at any moment she would adjust the fit of the wire-rimmed glasses she wore. He had noticed the change of spectacles the moment he'd seen her that evening. She had changed the wide-shouldered sheath dress for a sleek and classy blue one, and the sandals had been replaced by a pair of pumps that matched her outfit in color and style. But it was the gold frames of the new glasses that added the extra touch of class, the cool hint of mystery.

Sylvie Anne had dressed for him, whether she realized it or not. Her entire ensemble had been chosen to give the impression of inaccessibility, and Max could only assume she'd meant the message for him. But he was beginning to get other messages from Sylvie, little signals that he chose to interpret as a reciprocal interest. She'd go down in flames before admitting it, but he knew she was aware of it too. The very fact that she treated the whole thing as a joke appealed to his sense of humor. But there was a very real, very serious attraction operating below the surface . . . for both of them.

Max shifted position and caught Sylvie's glance. His eyes held hers in a brief but scintillating encounter. As she turned her head, her fingers moved to touch the wire frame of her glasses and Max felt a slow smile begin. He knew he was enjoying the early rituals of this flirtation far more than was prudent, but she was so delightfully indifferent, so careful to maintain that cut-above-the-rest composure. He couldn't resist the challenge. It was a flaw in his character, he supposed, but he was going to see just how deep Sylvie's resistance ran.

". . . and everything worked out just the way Sylvie Anne said it would, but there were a few anxious—" Juliette straightened and her eyes widened as she looked through the window. "Oh, there's John and Melissa. See? Out there on the sidewalk." She lifted her hand to wave. "You remember meeting them this afternoon, don't you, Sylvie? They have the bakery with the heavenly cookies."

Sylvie remembered, but didn't have time to comment before Juliette was pushing back her chair. Max got only halfway out of his own chair before Juliette was pushing him back down with a hand on his shoulder. "Don't get up, Max," she said. "I just want to tell Melissa something I forgot to. You and Sylvie stay put and I'll be right back."

Juliette left the table and Sylvie decided the ensuing silence had to be the high point of the evening. Even Max, as he settled back into a lazy posture, seemed to be absorbing the sudden quiet as if it were an afterdinner mint.

"Is it true?"

"That she'll be back?" Sylvie nodded wearily. "I'm afraid so."

His husky chuckle had a pleasant resonance, a soothing richness. "I meant is it true that you spiked the punch at the sophomore prom and then had to resuscitate Juliette's short basketball player?"

"Oh, Max, you didn't really listen to all that, did you?"

"Of course I listened." He paused, and his eyes darkened to a flirty velvet-blue. "After all, she was talking about you."

"And talking and talking. You shouldn't have encouraged her."

His grin was disarming. "You noticed that, huh?"

"Oh, I've been awake off and on all evening. Actually, Max, you got exactly what you deserved."

"I usually do, Sylvie Anne. You might want to remember that."

"I'll make a note in my diary just as soon as you break into the house and open the door." Sylvie tucked her hair behind her ear and glanced at the window. Juliette was outside on the sidewalk, chattering away, her hands moving up and down as she told Melissa whatever it was she had forgotten to tell that afternoon. With a sigh Sylvie looked back to Max.

"I still can't believe I forgot to get the key. It's usually the first thing I ask for whenever I'm staying with her. It doesn't matter which lock the key fits—house, car, file cabinet, or jewelry box—if it can be locked, Juliette can lose the key."

"I haven't noticed that she has too much of a problem with that sort of thing. As far as I know, you're the first person who's been locked out." He smiled. "Twice in one day, Sylvie. Maybe she's trying to tell you something."

Sylvie straightened her shoulders. "Maybe you just don't know everything that happens next door."

"This morning you seemed to think I knew quite a bit about it. Are you having a little trouble deciding on which side of the property line I belong?" He lifted his coffee cup and sipped, watching her all the while.

"I haven't given it much thought, but I do hope you'll stay on our side long enough to get the house unlocked."

"*Our?*"

With a shrug Sylvie took her napkin from her lap and placed it on the table. "I'm accustomed to using the plural possessive with Juliette. A habit left from when I lived at home, I suppose."

"Probably something similar to Juliette's habit of depending on you to remember the key."

Sylvie regarded him pensively. "I hardly think that could be called a habit. Juliette was excited about going out to dinner with you tonight and she simply forgot, that's all."

"And is that the reason you forgot the key, Sylvie Anne? Were you excited about being with me?"

"You should never ask a question like that, Max, unless you're prepared to hear an honest answer."

"I'm ready. Let's hear it."

"And spoil the mood of this entire evening with a bit of truth? No, I wouldn't want to do that."

"It's all right." He pushed back his chair and prepared to rise. "I know what you would have said." Standing, he came around the table to pull back her chair. "And I know it would have been a bit of the truth and a bit of a lie too. But I'd still like to know"— he smiled down at her—"if you spiked the punch."

She tucked her purse under her arm, picked up the embroidered clutch Juliette had left behind, and stood, facing Max. "The reports of my heroism are greatly exaggerated. I told you this afternoon you shouldn't believe everything Juliette says."

"I hope that holds true for you too." With a touch of his hand to her back he kept Sylvie beside him as he walked toward the counter and the waiting cashier. "The reports of my relationship with your sister have been exaggerated somewhat as well."

Sylvie wasn't in the mood for that kind of honesty. It wasn't any of her business, for one thing, and for another, it gave her a definite feeling of disloyalty. "I wouldn't worry too much about that, Max. Juliette falls in and out of love the way most people catch a cold. With the kind of attention you paid her during dinner, I'm sure she's already beginning to sniffle."

His lips curved just a little as he stopped to pay the check. Then, slipping his billfold into his hip pocket, he turned to face her. "I think you missed the point, Sylvie Anne. I was only listening to Juliette tonight. I was paying attention to *you.*"

"Then you've had a doubly wasted evening, Max."

"Maybe. Maybe not. I'm going to reserve judgment on that until later." He opened the door for her, and as she walked past him, her chin high, shoes tapping the floor in determined steps, her whole demeanor one of cool, impenetrable confidence, he knew he had to have the last word. "In the meantime, Sylvie, you might want to take a little extra vitamin C, yourself . . . just in case."

It was the most casually provocative statement any man had made to her in ages, and a fine thread of pleasure spun through her senses. Not that she believed he actually meant it, but still . . .

"No need for concern, Max. I have a natural immunity to the common cold."

"Oh, are we going?" Juliette waved to her friends and joined Sylvie and Max in front of the restaurant. "I was just getting ready to come inside." She took the purse Sylvie offered. "Thanks, Syl. And thank you for dinner, Max. It was great. Wasn't it, Sylvie?"

"Yes," she agreed. "Great."

Max smiled his acceptance of the overwhelming appreciation. "Would anyone like to go for a drive?" he asked.

"Let's!" Juliette clapped her hands, dropped her purse, and bent to retrieve it.

"Let's break into your house instead." Sylvie stopped to wait for Julie, but Max merely shortened his stride. "First things first."

"Well, afterward we can go for a drive." Juliette passed by Sylvie to catch up with Max.

"Not me," Sylvie said, although it seemed somewhat unnecessary. "The only place I'm going is to bed."

"Now that you mention it," Max observed, swinging an amused glance in Sylvie's direction, "bed sounds like a good place to be. We'll go for a drive another night, Julie. I think I might be coming down with something."

"Oh." Disappointment and concern blended in Juliette's voice, but Sylvie personally thought he was asking for trouble. "Well, I guess if you both . . ." Juliette turned her concern toward Sylvie. "You're not coming down with a cold or anything, are you?"

"Of course not." It was the most definite answer she'd ever given to that particular question, but she wanted to leave no doubt in Max's mind. Satisfied, she drew a deep breath of the clean, pine-scented air . . . and sneezed. Once and then again.

It was not, Sylvie realized, a good way to punctuate the conversation.

"Are you about to get it open?" Juliette leaned closer, peering over Max's shoulder as he tried to jimmy the window.

He sighed and slowly straightened. "Why don't you let Sylvie hold the flashlight for a while?"

"Oh, that's all right," Juliette assured him. "I'm not tired."

Max turned a look of appeal to Sylvie and she took pity on him. She rose to her feet from the low balustrade where she'd been sitting for the past twenty minutes while Juliette and Max had gathered the break-in equipment and gone to work on the window. So far there had been little progress, but then

Juliette was having a problem holding the light steady.

"Need some help?" Sylvie asked as she crossed the porch and took the flashlight from her sister. "I thought you were experienced with this sort of thing, Max. Why is it taking so long?"

"Nothing was said about experience or time requirements." He bent to the window again. "But I'm sure it would go faster if I didn't have to give on-the-job training to my accomplices in crime."

"Oh, my God," Juliette whispered, "I never thought of that."

"On-the-job training?" Sylvie asked.

"No, crime. What if we get arrested?"

"We'll show the arresting officer your driver's license or some kind of identification," Sylvie said as she tried to position the light so Max could see. "You'll think of something, Juliette. I've seen you explain your way out of situations that were more incriminating than this. Although if Max doesn't hurry—"

"Hold it steady, would you?" Max took hold of the flashlight and directed the beam at the sill.

"I don't have my license." Juliette leaned against the side of the house and began rummaging through her purse. "My billfold wouldn't fit. . . . Oh, wait, here's something." Paper rustled, but Sylvie didn't pay much attention. She just wanted to get the window opened, the door unlocked, and herself into bed.

"It's that letter," Juliette said. "I meant to tell you about this, Sylvie Anne. But after I read it, I stuck it in this purse and"—she bumped against Sylvie as she tried to hold the piece of paper toward the light—"I didn't think of it, again. It's—"

"Watch out, Juliette." Sylvie managed to keep the flashlight steady.

"What? Oh, sorry. It's from an attorney in Fayetteville about the house."

"This house?" Sylvie watched as Max carefully pried the window up a bare quarter of an inch.

"No. Hannah Lee House. The one we bought for the business. There's a"—she held the paper closer to the flashlight—"a lien on the property."

"What?" Sylvie turned the light to the paper. "A lien? Are you sure?"

"Hey! How am I supposed to—?"

Sylvie ignored Max's grumbling as she read the letter. "Benton Prestridge," she said when she'd finished. "You were supposed to contact him, Juliette. Did you, by any chance?" It was a foolish question, but Sylvie felt she ought to ask.

Juliette stiffened in a pose of self-defense. "I just found the letter again, Sylvie. How could I have contacted him?"

There was no point in asking how she had come to misplace the letter in the first place. "When did you receive it, Juliette?"

Max sighed in frustrated patience. "Look at the date, Sylvie. Then please hold the light so I can get this damned window open."

The flashlight beam flicked to the upper right-hand corner. "Two weeks ago. God, Juliette, didn't it occur to you . . . ?" Sylvie let the useless question fade and mimicked Max's sigh. "I'll phone him first thing in the morning."

She pointed the light downward and found Max frowning up at her, his eyes indigo in the darkness. "I thought the business belonged to Julie," he said.

"It does, but I—"

"Then let her take care of it."

Juliette folded the letter, her discomfort obvious in the noisy way she crumpled the paper. "That's right, Sylvie. Let me take care of this."

Sylvie had no idea how she had become the villain in the scheme of things, but Juliette certainly wasn't upset with Max for butting in. And she didn't seem overly upset with Mr. Benton Prestridge either. So that left Sylvie to take the blame. Max should have kept his unsolicited opinion to himself.

There was a splintery sound as the wooden sill released its hold, and then Max pushed open the window. "All right, Julie," he announced. "You can slip through the opening and go around to the front door."

"Thanks, Max." Juliette tugged at the front of her trouser legs before putting one foot over the sill and into the room on the other side. Once inside, she leaned out to smile in triumph. "I knew you could do it, Max."

Her voice was perfectly innocent, but it irritated Sylvie nonetheless. She resolved that she wouldn't, absolutely would not, feed his ego. Holding the flashlight steady and with equally steady intent, she reached to touch the sill and examine the damage done to the window frame.

"I'll fix that tomorrow." He straightened and moved away from her, and Sylvie wished she hadn't let her irritation goad her into such petty behavior. After all, what difference did a few scratches in the wood make? "Unless, of course"—he turned to her with a smile that in the darkness might have been teasing or challenging—"you want to take care of it for me."

Her hands clenched of their own accord, but she maintained her composure. "I took a class in wood refinishing once, but since you did the damage you can have the honor of repairing it."

A subtle tension steeped in the silence and Sylvie willed Max to give her an excuse, any excuse, for telling him what was on her mind. Instead, he picked up his tools, flipped the herringbone jacket over his arm, and walked to the end of the porch.

"A simple 'no, thank you' would have sufficed, Sylvie Anne." He stepped over the balustrade and started across the yard. Moonlight caught at the midnight dusk of his hair and then she couldn't see him at all. The door beside her opened and Juliette stood in the lighted hallway.

"About that letter, Sylvie Anne," she began hesitantly. "I'll call that man tomorrow, but I just—well, I need to know what, exactly, is a lien?"

"A lien is . . ." Sylvie tried to focus her attention on Juliette and the latest complication, but she couldn't seem to pull her eyes or her thoughts from the darkness on the other side of the balustrade. She wanted to apologize to Max, which was ridiculous, because she had done nothing to apologize for. *He* was the one who ought to apologize. He'd done all the teasing. He'd been goading her all evening with his flirty comments and seductive glances. He'd been the one to state an opinion that had been neither needed nor asked for.

But the apology stayed on her tongue and would not go away. So, all right, she would admit she had

overreacted—a little—but Max needed to understand about Juliette and the business and . . .

"Sylvie?"

"Hmm?"

"The lien?"

"I don't know, Juliette." Sylvie lifted her hand in a
distracted gesture. "Look it up in the dictionary or
something."

"I know what it *is*, Sylvie, I just don't know what it
means." Juliette paused. "What's wrong with you
anyway? Why don't you come inside? I've been holding this door—"

Sylvie turned in sudden decision. "I want to tell
Max something. When I get back, we'll talk about the
lien, all right?"

"Sure." Juliette frowned uncertainly. "Do you
want me to go over to his house with you?"

Sylvie shook her head. "I can handle Max."

"If you're not home by dawn, I'll know you did just
that." Juliette flashed her back-to-normal, saucy grin
and closed the door.

CHAPTER FIVE

Sylvie approached Max's house with brisk confidence, but she had a sudden awkward feeling as the front porch came into view and she saw him sitting on the top step. The house behind him was dark, but the moon illuminated the porch and Max with a silvery, dusky light. She was struck by the very real, very masculine appeal of his dark hair and blue eyes, his strong facial features, and the sense of inner security that seemed such a part of him.

"Well, hello, Miss Congeniality," he said. "Has she locked you out again? Or are you casing the neighborhood?"

Sylvie pressed her glasses firmly against her nose and forced herself to offer him a smile. "No, I came to —" The apology she had felt she ought to offer was nowhere to be found, snuffed out, she supposed, by his snippy greeting. "I came to tell you, Max, that no matter how you feel toward my sister, her business is none of yours. I'm here to help her set up the dress shop, and we do not need your advice or your opinions. I'd appreciate it if you'd keep that in mind."

"Hmm." He pursed his lips, thinking that if his hands hadn't already been clasped, he would have put them around her neck—tightly.

"Sit down, Sylvie." With a tilt of his head he indicated that she should sit beside him on the steps. "I think there are a couple of points here that need clarification."

She stood stubbornly at the base of the stairs and Max decided to bide his time and see what developed. He didn't think Sylvie would walk away from the chance to clarify anything. And if she did? Well, he would lay in a supply of crossword puzzles to challenge him through the winter. It would probably be a hell of a lot better for his mental health, not to mention his ego. But even as he toyed with the idea, he felt the tug of attraction and the certainty that she felt it too. Why else would she hesitate to sit beside him? Why else would she have followed him home?

He hid his smile as she moved, with self-assured steps, to sit next to him. Apparently, he thought, she'd decided that not sitting beside him would in some way incriminate her and make him think that she was afraid to sit beside him, which he did anyway. Max waited as she adjusted her feet, her dress, and her glasses to their respective and appropriate positions.

"All right, Max," she said crisply. "What points do you need clarified?"

"Oh, the clarification isn't for me, Sylvie. It's for you."

She didn't like that, he could tell by the tilt of her chin.

"Really?" she asked, her voice cooling by a degree or two.

"Really." He turned toward her, resting his back against the concrete column. "First point: my relationship with your sister. Clarification: I like Juliette.

I'd even go so far as to say I like her a lot. But that's as far as it goes, Sylvie. As far as it will ever go."

Sylvie crossed her arms, a sure indication of doubt, and Max tapped his hand against his leg. "I don't know what Juliette has told you, but—"

"Juliette has been my sister for quite some time, Max. I don't believe everything she says."

"You don't seem to believe me either."

She glanced at him and the faint shadow of amusement touched her lips. "Let's just say I've heard the this-is-as-far-as-it-goes line before. And from better men than you are, Gunga Din."

His lips curved, too, but his eyes held hers with an underlying truth. "Not better men, Sylvie Anne. Fools, if they were with you and talked only of your sister."

Sylvie laughed despite the tension closing around her throat. "Very prettily said, Max, but it lacks a certain something. Conviction, maybe."

"Conviction?"

Ignoring his soft echo, Sylvie continued. "And now that you've clarified for me just how you *don't* feel about Juliette, let's move on to—"

"I think the lack of conviction is all yours, Sylvie." The teasing quality was missing from his voice, the night shadows hid the expression in his eyes, and her heart began to beat an odd, unfamiliar pattern. "I think you're afraid to give the benefit of the doubt to any man who pays you a compliment. It's safer to believe that Juliette is the main attraction, isn't it?"

Sylvie did not want to answer. His question was too personal, too probing. And yet, she didn't want to give him the impression that she was afraid to answer. She hedged. "A profound observation, Max, but hardly pertinent to a discussion of Juliette's business."

" 'Juliette's business' is something of a misnomer, isn't it?"

"No. It's her idea, her responsibility, and her headache. I'm only here to—"

"Take care of the details. Yes, I remember." He watched Sylvie for a moment, watched the way she finger-combed a strand of hair behind her ear, watched the way she pretended not to watch him. "And where do the 'details' end and the responsibilities begin?"

"Juliette's young and inexperienced, Max. She needs my help in getting the shop set up, and I'd appreciate it if you wouldn't try to influence her."

"I've never tried to influence Julie. I'm not sure I could if I wanted to. She's never quiet that long."

"Oh, you could, Max. And you did. She saw you turn away two customers from your store this afternoon."

Max straightened, pulling away from the concrete support. "Now, wait just a minute, Sylvie Anne. I'm not going to keep my store hours according to *your* schedule. And I'm not about to apologize for it either."

"I was merely pointing out how you influence Juliette."

"Well, quite frankly, I don't see how anyone could have any influence on her when you're around to protect her from such gross business errors as closing a half hour early."

"You'll have to admit it isn't a good practice."

"I'll admit nothing of the kind. I'm not about to defend my right to run my shop in any way I please.

85

But I do think you ought to back off and give Juliette the same option."

"There's a right way and a wrong way—"

"So let Juliette discover that for herself. If it's her responsibility, then let her make some mistakes and take the consequences. How else is she going to learn? I'd be willing to bet you've never allowed anyone to protect you."

"I don't need protecting. I learned a long time ago to accept the consequences for my own actions." Her shoulder brushed against his as she straightened, and a warning tingled along her nerve endings. She'd been so intent on defending her position that she hadn't realized they were sitting so close together. Perhaps it was time to end the discussion. She didn't know why she'd bothered to argue with him anyway. His opinion didn't matter. With deliberately unhurried movements she got to her feet and smiled down at him in polite conclusion.

He smiled back and then rose easily. Standing, he moved closer to her, and the air felt heavy as she drew a long breath.

"No one could accuse you of lacking conviction, could they, Sylvie?"

She had the oddest impulse to deny it, to admit she wasn't sure about anything at the moment. But it was, she knew, nothing more than a passing thought. "No, Max. No one has ever accused me of not knowing my own mind. And I hope you're not about to become the first."

"I wouldn't dream of it."

His finger sketched a lazy path along his jaw, and Sylvie watched, knowing she ought to step away, unwilling to acknowledge the huskiness in his voice as a warning of his intention.

"It's refreshing to meet a woman who understands the consequences"—his finger touched her chin and skimmed along the curve of her mouth—"of standing in the moonlight."

She had time to turn away from the slow descent of his lips, she even had time to wonder why she didn't. His hands cupped her shoulders, but he didn't make any attempt to draw her into his arms, and in some distant corner of her thoughts Sylvie was glad. She would have felt obligated to protest, and she didn't want to do that. And it would be just a kiss, she told herself, probably a very casual sort of kiss at that. There was no point in letting him think she felt strongly about it either way.

But with the first gentle pressure of his mouth against hers, a subtle curiosity held her, a definite warmth enclosed her. Her heart hammered in her breast with all the anticipated excitement she had felt on the occasion of her very first kiss. The boy— she couldn't even remember his name—had been nervous and inexperienced. She had been left wondering what all the fuss was about.

Not so with Max. He wasn't nervous, and he certainly wasn't inexperienced. If she'd had any doubt about that, the tantalizing movement of his tongue along the outline of her lips dispelled it. And she . . . well, she thought she might wonder for some time to come about the sensations dancing like a newborn butterfly along her spine.

Sylvie had no intention of relaxing, but she did. Just a little, but enough to appreciate the feel of his muscular chest beneath her palms. When had she done that? She had no memory of placing her hands there, but there they were, and she reasoned that she might as well enjoy the benefits. After all, most of the men she knew from this perspective were not as tall, as broad, or as skilled as Max. She hated to admit that a man with whom she had nothing in common, a man who was not her type, could make a simple kiss seem special, could make her feel so delightfully feminine with just a touch.

His lips nudged hers, softly, with compelling persuasion, and she allowed the kiss to deepen ever so slightly. Allowed? She hadn't had a prayer of stopping her own quickening response. It really shouldn't go on, she realized, but her resistance was dizzy. Or dazed. Or defective. Whatever it was, it certainly wasn't putting up much of a fight.

Then, in sheer necessity, she pulled back, more to prove that she could than because she really wanted the caress to end. Max released her immediately, his hands lingering on her shoulders for only a moment before returning to his sides. In the dusky quiet her eyes met and held his, denying that she had felt anything out of the ordinary.

"Lovely." His voice was a throaty whisper, and as if it controlled her heartstrings, an uneven rhythm began pulsing through her veins. "Don't you agree, Sylvie Anne?"

On what, the kiss, the night? Her participation? Well, whatever he was asking her to confirm, she didn't think she ought to encourage him.

" 'Lovely' seems a bit strong," she said, and then paused to clear an inexplicable huskiness from her own voice. "Mildly pleasant would be a more apt description."

His brows arched with amusement. "I believe you're right. It's been a 'mildly pleasant' evening, Sylvie. From beginning to . . . end. Let's do it again soon." Max stepped up onto the porch and into the shadow of the house. "Thank you, Sylvie, for seeing me safely to my door."

Laughter coated his words, and her earlier annoyance with him wedged into her calm, collected, and cooling smile. "Think nothing of it, Max. I certainly don't." She stepped down onto the sidewalk. "And as for staging a repeat of this 'mildly pleasant' evening, we probably shouldn't push our luck."

Max chuckled. "Good night, Sylvie Anne. I'll see you tomorrow."

Not if she could do anything about it. The thought accompanied her as she walked toward Juliette's house and the lighted kitchen window. Sylvie sighed in resignation. Just what she needed. A sister who was lying in wait for her with instant cocoa, a legal entanglement, and a dozen questions about how she had handled Max.

Not a good way to end the evening. Not a good way at all.

The offices of Forsythe, Prestridge and Solomon were located in the heart of Fayetteville, or so Juliette said. Sylvie paid little attention to the landmarks her sister pointed out as Max drove through the town. She had paid little attention to anything on the trip from Eureka Springs other than the occupants of the car. Or more specifically, one occupant: Max.

It made her angry to think that for four whole days, she had scorned, ignored, and analyzed her reaction to him, all to no avail. There was no logical explanation for her inability to get him out of her thoughts. Since the midnight kiss she'd seen him twice, and both occasions had been brief and at a distance. He'd called her name, waved, and gone about his business. He'd told Juliette he was busy when she'd phoned to invite him to dinner the next day. He'd been expecting an important telephone call the day after that.

That Max would resort to worn-out excuses after only one kiss, and a rather casual kiss at that, struck Sylvie as being funny . . . and a little humbling as well. Not that she cared. By avoiding her he had saved her the trouble of flatly telling him she was not interested. And it had saved her hours of frustration in convincing Juliette there was no future in playing matchmaker. Still, Sylvie didn't like this avoidance therapy. After such a display of outrageous flirtation he should have tapered the game to a dignified end, not dropped it like a hot potato.

But she could hardly complain. At least not until she'd discovered earlier that morning that Max was driving her and Juliette to Fayetteville. He'd knocked at the kitchen door, announced that it was time to leave, and escorted them to his car. Her initial irritation had soon blended with another when Sylvie realized that neither Juliette nor Max was going to offer any explanation for his presence on this trip that was supposed to be strictly business, and Juliette's business at that. Sylvie had broached the subject to her sister before getting into the car and been told that Max had business in town too. There wasn't much she could say after that, but she couldn't help wondering . . . and wondering.

From beneath suspiciously narrowed lashes she looked at him now. Taking a seat in one of the chairs in the reception area of the Forsythe, Prestridge and Solomon office, Max appeared quite comfortable. He was dressed casually, of course, in a denim shirt, blue jeans, and deck shoes. It wasn't an unattractive combination. Sylvie admitted that he looked somewhat appealing, but she did think he should have worn something more suitable for a business meeting. But then she had no idea what sort of business he intended to conduct.

She dropped her gaze to the magazine in her lap and turned a page with listless interest. Juliette should have been back by now. She shouldn't have left, after they'd parked in front of the law office, to run an errand in the first place. But, in typical Juliette fashion, she'd turned a deaf ear to Sylvie's caution and promised it would take only a minute; then she'd departed, leaving Sylvie and Max to wait for the scheduled appointment.

Sylvie turned another page and glanced at her watch.

"You don't really expect her to be back here anytime soon, do you?" Max laid aside the magazine he'd been leafing through.

With great forbearance she refrained from frowning at him. "Of course I expect her back. Don't you?"

"Not until you've had time to take care of this little detail for her." He held up his hand to prevent an interruption. "Don't get me wrong. Juliette intended to be here in plenty of time for the appointment and she'll have a perfectly logical explanation for the delay. At least, it will be perfectly logical to her. But you know as well as I do that she'll be late."

Sylvie did know . . . but it annoyed her that Max should point it out. "Don't feel obligated to wait on my account, Max. If you have something else to do, please be my guest."

"No problem," he said with that irritatingly easygoing smile. "There's nothing I'd rather do than wait here with you, Sylvie Anne."

Oh, please, she thought, but she held back the rising sigh of frustration. "I'm sure that's true, but since you do have business in town—"

"Juliette took my car, and I'm in no hurry anyway. Besides, Sylvie, if I left, who would hold your hand?"

"The list is endless, but if I run out of possibilities, I'll let you know."

His smile tilted upward, undaunted. "I think that list needs to be updated. Would you like me to take care of it for you?"

She laughed because it suddenly seemed the easiest response. "It would serve you right, Max, if I took you up on that."

"Yes, I have a feeling it would." He looked unconcerned by the prospect, even a bit hopeful of being put to the test, and Sylvie felt a thread of anticipated pleasure curl tightly inside her. She pulled her gaze from his and settled her glasses more securely in place. As the door to an inner office opened, she looked up.

"Ms. Smith?"

Benton Prestridge looked to be in his early thirties. He was not too tall, and a bit on the lean side, but his appearance was—to Sylvie—close to perfect. His hair was sandy-blond, his eyes were brown, and his pinstripe suit could have come straight from Boston. Sylvie smiled, stood, and crossed the reception area. "I'm Sylvie Smith."

"Benton Prestridge." He shook her hand, acknowledging the introduction with a firm, professional warmth. "Won't you come into my office?"

"My sister, Juliette, made the appointment, Mr. Prestridge, but she's been delayed. If it's all right, I can—"

"Oh, of course." He held open the opaque glass door in invitation and allowed Sylvie to enter the office. "That will be fine. In fact, I don't have a lot of time. I'm due in court—"

The door closed on the rest of the sentence and Max frowned his general opinion of Fayetteville attorneys. He caught the inquisitive gaze of the woman at the front desk and smiled somewhat self-consciously.

"Would you like some coffee?" the secretary asked.

"No, thank you." He picked up the discarded magazine and shuffled the pages, searching for his place.

"They won't be long. Mr. Prestridge is very conscientious about court appearances." The secretary turned her attention to the folder in her hand, and Max wondered whether she'd been trying to reassure him as to Sylvie's safe return or the attorney's adherence to punctuality. Not that he was particularly worried on either count. Max didn't care one way or the other whether Benton Prestridge was late for a court appearance. And Sylvie Anne was more than capable of handling a mere lawyer.

Max scanned an advertisement for men's cologne and flipped the page to an article on an upcoming documentary on the bald eagle. He wondered if Sylvie was interested in the plight of endangered species. More to the point, he wondered if she'd be interested to know that *he* was interested. Probably not, but he honestly couldn't be sure.

He had done a lot of thinking about Sylvie in the past four days, a lot more than he'd intended. There had been too much time to think about her, for one thing. With Miriam gone, he had been at the store more than usual. Luckily, the season was winding to a halt and in another few weeks he could close the shop for the winter. Usually, that meant trading one hectic schedule for another, but not this year. This year he'd planned to spend the winter months in Eureka, working on a few of the projects for which he never seemed to have enough time. This year he'd planned to relax, enjoy the fruits of his labor. But that, of course, had been his idea before Juliette moved next door.

Max idly turned the pages of the eagle story. Juliette Smith was an endangered species, he decided. A bird with a broken wing, eliciting both sympathy and affection, destined always to need someone or something. She was, admittedly, a charming nuisance, delightful in small doses, but a nuisance just the same. And just when he'd resigned himself to having a small blond crisis next door, Sylvie had arrived.

A diversion, he'd thought that first day. An attractive, intelligent, independent woman who made it quite obvious that she wasn't looking for romance. But the problem was, although she wasn't looking, she was vulnerable to it. He'd suspected it, but he'd known for certain when he kissed her. That kiss had put a different perspective on the game, at least in his mind, and in all the time he'd spent thinking about it, he couldn't decide who was in the more vulnerable position, he or Sylvie.

". . . so it shouldn't be too complicated to have the lien removed. But it will take time."

Max heard the soothing assurances as the inner office door opened. Sylvie stepped through the doorway, followed by Benton Prestridge, who was talking and smiling at the same time. Sylvie was smiling, too, and Max felt a nagging discontent stir to life inside him. Sooner or later she would smile like that for him. Game or no game, he wasn't going to quit until she did.

"Oh, am I late?" Juliette entered through the wide front doorway of the office and moved forward, her whole demeanor one of innocent apology. "I'm sorry, Sylvie. The car stalled and it wouldn't—I don't know what happened, Max, but . . ."

Sylvie could well imagine what had happened. Juliette had a lead foot and flooded the engine as often as not. Max should have known better than to let her use his car, anyway. Sylvie glanced at him, still seated in the chair, apparently still comfortable, and showing tremendous patience by not demanding to know if the car was outside in the law firm's parking lot or if it had been towed to the nearest police station. Not that he was likely to receive an answer anytime soon, Sylvie thought as she glanced at her sister. Juliette was lost in her own little scenario, staring at Benton Prestridge as if he were a five-pound box of Godiva chocolates.

"Hello," Juliette murmured. "You must be the one . . ."

"Yes." Benton stepped forward as if in a daze and Sylvie had to bite her lip to keep from laughing aloud.

". . . who wrote the letter," Juliette continued, although it was obviously an unnecessary clarification.

"It was my pleasure." As Benton took Juliette's hand in a clasp that didn't even resemble a professional handshake, Sylvie looked to Max to share her amusement. His lips curved in answer and she was glad, suddenly very glad, that he was nearby.

"A match made in heaven," Max observed dryly.

"And set aflame in Arkansas," Sylvie agreed as Max leaned back, placing his arm along the back of her chair. A pleasant warmth wrapped around her shoulders, although he didn't actually touch her. The feeling might have been her imagination, or maybe she just was experiencing a vicarious heat from the couple on the dance floor. Juliette and Benton were generating enough warmth to heat Fayetteville for months.

It had been a matter of ten to fifteen minutes, certainly no longer than that, between Juliette's late arrival at the law office and Benton's won't-take-no-for-an-answer invitation to dinner. And he'd known just the place, a private club with live music and an insignificant cover charge. Sylvie had raised her eyebrows at that, fairly certain that such a suggestion was not standard treatment for clients of Forsythe, Prestridge and Solomon. Max's reaction had been more to the point: *"How* insignificant?" he'd asked. Juliette had accepted graciously for everyone present, arranged time, place, and transportation, and forestalled the possibility of argument by saying that that would give the mechanic who'd rescued her in the middle of the intersection plenty of time to check Max's car.

"Would you like to dance?" Max put his lips close to

Sylvie's ear. "Rogers and Astaire out there are leaving plenty of room for us amateurs."

"Amateur? Speak for yourself." Sylvie watched the almost nonexistent dance steps of the only couple on the floor. Blond head was bent to blond curls and Juliette was laughing up at Benton. "Do you suppose they have any idea what time it is?"

"Do you honestly think it would make a difference if they did?" His fingers brushed against her shoulder in a reassuring pat. "Relax, Sylvie Anne. Julie seems quite capable of falling in love without your assistance."

Sylvie turned to Max, arching her brows in succinct skepticism. "Love at first sight? Come on, Max. I know you're too intelligent to believe that."

"What does intelligence have to do with it?" His smile came with a low rustle of amusement. "Case in point—"

"My sister." Sylvie pushed her glasses into place and noticed that even with the cozy shadows surrounding the table, Max's eyes were an intense, recognizable blue. "This sort of thing happens to Juliette all the time. She walks into a room and the men form a line to the right."

"You'll notice I've been careful to stay on her left all evening."

"You can't take credit for that. Benton has had her pretty well covered from all angles." Sylvie let her gaze stray to the dance floor and pensively return to Max. "I'll confess that when I met him, I didn't think he would be so susceptible. He isn't really Juliette's type."

"I had the distinct impression this afternoon that you thought Benton was *your* type."

Sylvie shrugged and again felt the warmth of Max's arm along her shoulders. "Sometimes I'm more nearsighted with my glasses than without them." A soft breath of laughter escaped her and she wondered, fleetingly, if she'd had more than one glass of wine. "Juliette says pinstripes create a blinding glare in the lens."

Max furrowed his brow. "Makes sense to me. You ought to listen to her, Sylvie."

"Oh, sure. Then I'd be up to my eyebrows in"— God! She'd almost said "denim." Wouldn't Max have loved that?—"trouble," she substituted after a pause only a mother would have noticed. "Taking Julie's advice always means Trouble, with a capital *T*."

"And what kind of advice has she been offering you lately?" He moved closer, just a little, but his arm was undeniably around her now.

Sylvie decided not to notice. "Lately?" Pursing her lips as if she were trying to remember, she wondered what he would say if she told him the truth. "She's been trying to match me with you."

He smiled. "With no better luck than I'm having, obviously."

"You're not really trying very hard, Max."

"Would it be worth the effort?"

"Effort always makes one a better person."

He began to rub her shoulder in a smooth, massaging caress. "You're a tease, Sylvie Anne."

"Only after two glasses of wine."

"You've only had one."

"Then it must be the intoxicating company I keep." She knew she ought to order coffee or at least move away from his seductive touch, but it was relaxing and . . .

The warmth of his breath against her cheek was her first hint that Max had misinterpreted her comment. His lips brushed hers, lightly, and she thought perhaps he had done an excellent job of interpretation after all. The kiss was evanescent, hardly long enough to interfere with her pulse rate, but her heart didn't seem to understand. Like a hummingbird, it fluttered madly against her rib cage, creating an intriguing sort of panic. When he moved back, she moistened her lips and released a long, deep breath. "I don't care what you say, *someone* has been refilling my wineglass."

"You've been dating the wrong men, Sylvie, if they have to resort to getting you drunk."

"No one has ever tried to do that," she said, and then paused to consider. "My God, you're right. I have been dating the wrong men."

Max settled back in his chair, but his arm stayed around her shoulders. "Very funny, but probably closer to the truth than you think."

"The truth, Max, is that I don't think much about it either way. I'm not like Juliette. I don't fall in love on the basis of a handshake. I'm not looking for a relationship, so consequently, dating the 'wrong' man doesn't cause me to lose any sleep."

"Has any man?"

Sylvie knew what he meant, but she feigned innocence. "That's a rather personal question. I haven't asked you anything like that."

"If you did, I'd tell you I've never lost any sleep because of a man."

His smile teased her and the corners of her mouth lifted in response. "Well, neither have I."

The music ended with a smattering of lukewarm

applause from the dwindling number of listeners. Sylvie clapped her hands in belated and halfhearted acknowledgement. Max didn't bother and neither did Juliette and Benton. They stood, close together on the dance floor, talking and waiting, Sylvie supposed, for the music to begin again. They seemed in no hurry to bring the evening to an end, and Sylvie frowned at her own restlessness. It was Max, she decided. Max and the way he talked to her, the way he'd kissed her, that made her feel unsettled, even a little reckless.

She turned toward him in sudden decision, ready to trade the disquieting tone of their conversation for the uncertainty of being in his arms on the dance floor. Max was watching her, his expression oddly serious.

"Why don't we show Adam and Eve how to trip the light fantastic?" she suggested, but the words came out breathy and uneven.

Max nodded and stood, keeping his hand on the back of her chair as she rose. "Tell me, Sylvie," he asked softly, "what are you going to do if a relationship comes looking for you?"

His warm breath stirring against her hair, and his husky voice, created a subtle ache inside her. She denied the significance of both with a nonchalant lift of her shoulders. "I suppose I'd start losing sleep. Not an appealing prospect."

"Oh, I don't know. There could be certain advantages in that."

As they walked toward the dance floor, Sylvie shot him a teasing look over her shoulder. "Positive thinking is your forte, isn't it, Max?"

He turned her into his arms. "Among many other things, Sylvie Anne."

Dancing was one of them, Sylvie decided within a few minutes. His steps were smooth and effortless, and the deliberate distance she maintained seemed awkward and unnecessary. With a soundless sigh she relaxed into the rhythm of the music and the pleasant discovery that he was hardly an amateur.

"You constantly surprise me," she said with a smile. "I would never have guessed you'd spent your adolescent Saturday afternoons at Miss Wattenbarger's School of Dance."

"In my hometown in Kansas, it was Miss Harper, Miss Harpy to those in the know, and there wasn't a boy within fifty miles who would have stepped foot inside her studio." Max smiled wryly at the memory. "Lisa had no qualms, though, about sharing what she was taught. It was one of her favorite pastimes. Actually, I learned all I know about dancing under duress."

"Lisa?"

"Mmm. A redhead, like you."

"My hair isn't red," Sylvie corrected with unnecessary firmness, "it's nutmeg blond."

Max pulled back to look. "Oh," he said dubiously. "Well, Lisa's is the same color, but hers is red."

Sylvie ignored that. "Was she your first love?"

"Worse. My sister."

"I didn't know you had a sister." It was an inane statement, and Sylvie frowned as she said it.

"There are a lot of things you don't know about me, Sylvie Anne." He pulled her close, but she had the oddest impression that he kept an intangible distance between them, as if he resented the fact that she didn't seem to want to know more about him.

Her question came involuntarily in response. "Tell me, Max, how have you escaped?"

"Escaped?"

"A serious relationship," she explained. "Why aren't you involved in a matter of the heart?"

He looked down at her, but his expression and his smile were mysterious. "What makes you think I'm not?"

CHAPTER SIX

Max's question did keep Sylvie awake for some time that night, and it was her first conscious thought the next morning. Then, like an annoying commercial jingle, it occurred to her at odd moments throughout the day . . . and that night and the next morning. It didn't mean anything, Sylvie told herself, it just was a moment that for some reason had stuck in her memory.

By the end of the week it had become a litany of sorts, a ritual that passed through her mind several times before she fell asleep at night and a riddle to start her thoughts percolating first thing in the morning. *What makes you think I'm not?* She had laughed at the time and said she could tell by the way he parted his hair. But it had made her wonder about the type of woman Max would find attractive. He seemed to find *her* interesting. After all, he'd kissed her. Twice.

Ridiculous. The whole thing was ridiculous. She didn't care whether or not he was romantically involved with someone. As long as he wasn't involved with Juliette and/or Juliette's business, Sylvie was content to let Max do whatever he pleased.

That line of reasoning lasted for two weeks before

Sylvie admitted it was frayed from constant repetition. Max *was* doing what he pleased and she *wasn't* content. It pleased Max to spend time with her, wherever she chose to be. At first he gave, and Sylvie accepted, such blatant excuses as "Since Juliette has a date with Benton, you'll need company" and "My television gets lousy reception on that station. Do you mind if I watch the movie with you?" After the first week, though, he didn't bother with explanations . . . he just was always around.

"Of course I *like* him, Juliette. That isn't the point." Sylvie sat on the bed and watched as Juliette dabbed a touch of scent, about ten dollars' worth, Sylvie guessed, behind her ears.

"Then what is the point, Sylvie? You like Max. Max likes you. What could be better?"

It was the kind of simplistic logic that gave Sylvie a headache, but like it or not, there was an element of truth in Juliette's argument. And, unbelievably, Juliette seemed to realize it too.

"That's it, isn't it, Syl? The reason you want me to cancel my date with Benton tonight is not because you want to spend time with me, but because you don't want to spend time with Max."

Sylvie sighed and rubbed her forehead. "Julie, it's been two weeks since you met Benton Prestridge and every night since, he's been here or you've driven there. And when you couldn't manage either of those options, you spent three hours on a long-distance telephone conversation. I'm not asking for equal time, just one evening."

"To talk business." Juliette stared hard into the mirror as she clipped an earring into place. "I know you, Sylvie. You want to get started on the plans for the dress shop. Well, I do too. But Benton says . . ."

Sylvie thought it prudent to tune out the rest. Juliette could justify anything. And when she was in love, she generally did. All in all Sylvie could only blame herself for bringing up the subject of Max and his more or less constant presence. Now she had to acknowledge the hidden verity of Juliette's accusation. If she were really distressed by the amount of time Max spent keeping her company, Sylvie knew she would have put her foot down, slammed the door in his face, and let the telephone go unanswered.

But she did like him. Max was good company. Easy to be with and able to carry on an intelligent conversation, a commodity in short supply around the Smith household lately. Every time Juliette opened her mouth, Benton's name popped out. And an inseparable part of the problem with Max was that Sylvie was often left on her own to while away evening after evening in a strange town among strangers. Except for one. Max kept her from being lonely, but, perversely, Sylvie resented it. Loneliness made her vulnerable. And Max, in the most innocuous ways and with the utmost charm, was taking advantage of that.

"I knew right away that you and Max would . . ." The sentence dangled while Juliette pursed her lips, retouched a spot with pale-pink lip gloss, and narrowed her eyes to examine the overall effect. "Do you think this is all right?" She turned to Sylvie, her blue eyes harboring serious doubts. "Benton has never said anything specific, but I know he doesn't like bright lipstick applied with a heavy hand." Her dimples appeared with mischievous delight. "He prefers wash-and-wear shades that don't stain his shirt collar."

"I'm glad to hear he's still wearing a shirt on your dates."

Juliette wrinkled her nose. "Just because you and Max—"

"—are planning to run away and live together on a deserted beach in California is no reason for you to change your plans." Sylvie slid to the end of the bed and smiled benignly at her sister.

"You're absolutely right, Sylvie Anne. I think I hear Benton's car even as we speak. Doesn't he have the most wonderful sense of timing?" Juliette walked to the bedroom door, where she stopped, pirouetted gracefully, and allowed the mischief back into her eyes. "Send a postcard as soon as you're settled in, Syl. I can see it now—Max, wrapped in terry cloth, standing beside a tiny, but big enough, grass hut."

"Forget the hut, Juliette, it will be an old Victorian house that you will vaguely remember as being *yours*."

"That isn't nice, Sylvie. But I'm feeling magnanimous just now, so I swear on the key to my diary that we'll spend tomorrow working. There, how's that?"

She looked so pleased with herself that Sylvie didn't have the heart to tell her how, exactly, that was. With a sigh she stood. "Good night, Julie. Have fun."

Juliette became suddenly serious. "Listen, Sylvie, anytime you need to talk like this . . . well, I don't mind. In fact, I probably get more out of these sisterly chats than you do."

Of that, at least, Sylvie was certain.

"It's a phase, Max." Sylvie locked the door and stepped back to admire the stained glass inset, as she did each time she entered or left the old Victorian house. She was leaving now, having spent the day steaming, scraping, and squinting at a section of bedroom wallpaper, trying to decipher the original color and print. Renovation was definitely a challenge, one she hadn't planned on tackling alone. "Juliette will get tired of Benton's strict ideas about how the world should be run. Or he'll get bored with her impulsive disregard for propriety."

"That's probably why he canceled his afternoon appointments and took Juliette to the War Eagle Arts and Crafts Show," Max agreed, tongue in cheek. "Lucky thing I'm not bored with you, Sylvie. I might have taken you to War Eagle."

She frowned her lack of appreciation for his sense of humor. "Lucky for you, I had work to do. Not everyone," she said with a pointed look, "can afford to idle away the day dispensing unsolicited advice."

He held his hands palms up as he waited for her to join him at the bottom of the stairs. "Not everyone knows someone so desperately in need of advice."

"I thought we agreed not to discuss Juliette's lack of interest in restoring the house."

"You agreed, Sylvie. I cast my vote for not discussing Juliette at all."

He touched her arm as they turned together and began walking down Main Street toward home. Max touched her often, and Sylvie had finally stopped protesting. It wasn't, she reasoned, anything serious. His touch, as well as his occasional kiss, were too casual to make a protest worthwhile. He would only tease her, ask her why it bothered her, and that was a discussion she wished to avoid.

"Then why are we having this conversation?" she asked.

He grinned. "Because you think if you keep talking I'll forget that you owe me dinner."

"I seem to owe you dinner three out of four nights."

"And I do appreciate it. If you weren't such a lousy backgammon player, I might starve."

"If I weren't so easy, Max, I wouldn't let you win in the first place."

His smile tightened a bit at the corners. "You're many things, Sylvie Anne, but easy is not one of them."

Max entered The Attic through the back door and sniffed the unmistakable aroma of brewing coffee. Miriam, as usual, had come in early.

"Hi," she said as she pushed aside the doorway curtain that separated the workroom from the rest of the store. "I didn't expect to see you so early. Guilty conscience?"

He took off his coat, hung it on a hook, and turned to look at his assistant. Miriam Rogers was a former schoolteacher from Albuquerque who had retired to Eureka Springs with her husband. She'd begun working with Max the first month he'd opened the store and he'd had reason to thank his lucky stars for her ever since. Her personality was as bright as a newly minted penny and her cheery common sense was worth more than any salary could buy. She was tall, slender, elegant, and ageless. And she knew more about him than he'd ever willingly confided to his own mother.

"You're looking great, Miriam. Must have been a wild weekend at War Eagle."

"Wet is the word, Max. It was rainy, muddy, and awful, not necessarily in that order." She placed a narrow strip of lace on the workbench and retrieved a pencil from behind her ear. "If I hadn't seen Henry Casey and Grace and Greta Amos, it would have been a wasted trip. I sold one doll, one wooden truck, and told some woman the entire history of the Passion play. Can you believe that?"

"Sounds like a typical arts and crafts show to me. Anytime you say the word, Miriam, you can stop making the circuit of the annual fairs. We don't have to do that anymore. At first, those contacts and the few sales we made were important, but you know as well as I—"

"I know, Max, but I like to complain about them as much as I like to attend them. Where else can I get together with old cronies like Henry and the Amos sisters? Where else would anyone consider me an authority on the Passion play? I know you don't need the exposure, but I suppose I do. However, if I come down with pneumonia this week, I'm sending you the doctor bills."

Max settled onto a stool and studied the porcelain body of a ready-to-be-assembled doll. It was going to be Merlin, a part of the King Arthur's Court series of limited edition dolls. It was a project that Max had envisioned years before and had finally begun sculpting. But now he couldn't seem to remember where he'd left off. Sylvie, although she wasn't anywhere around, was distracting him.

"How are things at the restoration site?" Miriam asked, divining his train of thought as intuitively as Merlin might have divined King Arthur's.

"Progressing," he answered. "Sylvie says there's no point in delaying the work simply because of a legal technicality. The lien, according to Prestridge, is just an inconvenience and will be dismissed as soon as the Erikson-estate dispute is settled. I suppose Sylvie's right to continue the renovation—one way or another, it will have to be done."

"So that's how you spent your time while I was holding an umbrella at War Eagle."

He shrugged a sheepish admission. "How did you guess?"

She made a broad sweep of the room with one hand. "You never leave the workroom this neat, Max. You didn't even open the shop while I was gone, did you?"

"No one was in town, anyway."

"Save your reasons for Sylvie. Personally, it would suit me fine if you closed for the season today and devoted all your energy toward . . ." Bending her head, Miriam let the sentence fade into ambiguity as she began to pin the lace to a tiny satin dress. "I suppose," she said after a minute or two, "that Juliette and Benton are still an item?"

"You suppose right, Miriam. Sylvie swears it's just a passing infatuation, but I think it's serious. And every day Julie leaves something else for Sylvie to handle. I don't know how she manages to keep her cool."

Miriam smiled around the pins she held between her lips. "Sylvie assumes responsibility regardless of the circumstances. Besides, she has you to counteract the frustration she must be feeling toward her sister."

Max lifted Merlin's hand and examined the detail against the light. "Yes, I guess Sylvie does have me." A weighty frustration began pressing on his good humor. "The question is, what is she going to do with me?"

Miriam's laughter rang out rich and mellow. "Oh, I think the question is, what do you *want* her to do?"

Max thought a lot about that during the next few days. He'd begun the relationship with Sylvie—if it could be called a relationship—because he was restless and she offered a challenge. Someone new to talk with, to argue with, and to tease on occasion, nothing complicated. He had thought Sylvie would add a touch of laughter, a bit of spice, to an otherwise uneventful season. And she had. Totally, it seemed, against her better judgment.

And that, he decided, was what both puzzled and intrigued him. Sylvie enjoyed the time they spent together as much as he did. She even admitted it, but there was an element of waiting in her response, as if she expected him to tell her it was all a joke, that he'd just wanted to see how far the game could stretch before they both had a good laugh about it.

Max didn't understand her reaction, but he knew the game had progressed past the point of laughter. If, indeed, there ever had been a point at which he could have laughed about his . . . relationship . . . with Sylvie. He didn't know how to reach past her protective layer of sophistication, and he wasn't sure what to expect if he did. But he knew that, whatever reservations she had about his sincerity, she was attracted to him. And he knew that eventually her attraction would take a serious turn. Until then, Max had little choice but to wait and see what developed.

"Did you miss me?" Max sank onto the couch, cupped his hands at the back of his head, and settled his canvas-clad feet on the corner of the coffee table.

Sylvie frowned at the scene of contentment and pushed his feet off the edge so she could get past him and sit at the other end of the couch.

"Actually," she said, "I did miss you. Spending Thanksgiving at Dad's is always a trial, but add the world's most devoted couple, Juliette and Benton, and it becomes a real endurance test. I wished several times that you'd been able to come with us. There were some moments . . ." She rolled her eyes toward the ceiling. "Honestly, Max, you wouldn't have believed the conversation during Thanksgiving dinner. I think that's when I missed you most. I certainly needed your sense of the ridiculous then."

She wasn't serious, Max knew. But just the idea that she had associated a feeling of need with him was encouraging. He wished he had spent the holiday in Oklahoma with the Smiths, but he'd gone to his sister's in Louisville. And he'd missed Sylvie, more than he'd thought possible. He glanced over at her. She appeared relaxed and comfortable. Max wondered what she would do if he leaned across the cushions and kissed her, a long, sensuous, serious kiss. He'd like to think she would respond, but he could more easily imagine her pushing him away with a laugh and a quit-kidding-around scold.

"How was your holiday?"

"Noisy." Max again propped his feet on the coffee table. "Mom asked about you."

"Your mom?" *Stupid question*, Sylvie thought. And silly to be pleased at the knowledge that Max had mentioned her to his family. "Why would she do that?"

"She's always interested in the people I meet, especially when I spend a lot of time talking about them."

"Your holiday is beginning to sound as boring as mine." Sylvie adjusted her glasses and ran a weary hand through her hair. "I take that back. It wasn't boring, it was just redundant. Dad had to have every other word repeated because he won't wear his hearing aid, and Juliette, who knows better, missed all the words in between because her 'heart was listening to Benton's heart.'" Sylvie turned a wry smile toward Max. "Really, Max, you should have been there."

"Where's Julie now?"

"Upstairs. On the phone, probably. After all, it's been almost three hours since she saw him."

"Oh, come on, Sylvie Anne. There are worse things than being in love."

"Name one."

"Being in business with your sister."

"All right. Try for two."

"Did you get a chance to talk to her about the work that needs to be done? I thought you were definitely going to make an opportunity for discussion."

"I intended to, Max, but there wasn't enough time."

"Sylvie, you can't go on making all the decisions and hoping Juliette is going to redevelop an interest in opening the dress shop. She's going to have to face up to the responsibility of starting her own business sooner or later."

"We've had this conversation before, Max. Last week and the week before and the week before that. I'll tell you now what I told you then: I'll—"

"—take care of it." He held up his hands in surrender. "Okay, okay. Guess what we're going to do this week."

Sylvie tucked her feet beneath her and reclined lazily against the sofa arm. "I'm working. I couldn't begin to guess what you'll be doing."

"*You*, Miss Smith, and I are going on the Christmas Candlelight Tour of Homes and also to the Community Theater's annual production of *A Christmas Carol*. No arguments, please. Or else . . ."

"Or else what?"

"I won't help you with your wallpaper project this week."

Sighing in mock distress, Sylvie shook her head. "You're confusing me with my sister. I can manage quite well without your assistance this week. Besides, all you do is point out that Juliette should be the one working, something I'm well aware of."

"Every job needs a supervisor, you know."

"So you've told me. Forget what I said before, Max," she said dryly. "I didn't miss you after all."

"That's all right." He reached across the sofa cushion to cover her hand with a warmly tender touch. "I missed you enough for both of us."

She didn't know what to say. He was teasing, wasn't he?

Satisfied with catching her momentarily off guard, Max patted her hand, slipped his feet from the edge of the table, and stood.

"Don't forget, Sylvie, we have a date. You can

choose the night, providing it's Saturday, and I'll provide the candles."

"Should I bring a match?" she asked with a droll smile.

"A match made in heaven?"

"No, just the ordinary kitchen variety."

"Ah, who needs it?" With that he walked to the door and opened it. "Good night, Sylvie Anne. Pleasant dreams."

"Max?" She couldn't control the impulse that made her call to him. And she couldn't prevent herself from asking, "Are you really going to help me with the wallpaper?"

He grinned. "Oh, I'll be around."

As the door closed softly behind him, Sylvie sank back against the sofa arm. Around. Max was always around. Tampering with this, helping with that, telling her she was doing more than her share of Juliette's work and taking care of too many details. She resented his interfering, although she acknowledged his point. And she resented always having him around, although she would have to admit that she was learning to like it.

With a forefinger and thumb she adjusted the fit of the tortoiseshell frames on the bridge of her nose. The problem was—she sighed. She didn't know what the problem was. She wanted to feel indifferent toward him; she didn't. She didn't want to like him; she did. She wished he would stop teasing her in that half-sensuous, half-serious way.

But she didn't know why.

CHAPTER SEVEN

December arrived with the crisp, clean scent of winter, and, overnight it seemed, the town wrapped itself in Christmas colors. Downtown buildings donned the gay trappings of a Victorian Yule and the air was rich with spicy fragrances and the sound of carols. It took longer to walk from one end of Spring Street to the other, simply because the handmade decorations and holiday store windows along the way were too enticing. Sylvie found herself stopping time and again to admire a white oak basket with a big plaid bow that decorated the sidewalk in front of an antique store. And in the candy-shop window, atop a miniature tree, there was a gossamer angel made with delicate detail and a lacy design.

Max said it was made of sugar, spun by an elf, sculpted by fairies, and hung up to dry in the moonlight. Sylvie said it was crocheted by human hands, if not in direct sunlight, at least beneath a one-hundred-watt bulb.

But the magic slipped beneath the surface of her practical nature and urged her to purchase several brightly patterned bows, the white oak basket, and various other decorations. Sylvie surprised herself by obeying the impulse, but Max merely smiled.

He helped her drape garlands along the porch railing of the old Victorian house and it was his idea to place a single candle in the window. Inside, the house still bore the imprint of a renovation in progress, but on the outside it looked as finished and welcoming as any of the other restored homes in the town.

Juliette got into the Christmas spirit one day by dressing in a turn-of-the-century gown and putting a bit of mistletoe in her hair and around the house. As usual, she overdid the idea, but she looked so delightfully Victorian and was so pleased with herself that Sylvie didn't have the heart to remind her there was still plenty of work to be done.

On Saturday morning Sylvie awakened early with a sense of expectancy. She didn't know if it had more to do with Juliette's announcement the night before that she wanted to get an early start on painting the baseboard in the front room of the dress shop or Max's plans for the evening. Either way, Sylvie had no intention of dwelling on a simple feeling of anticipation. Yet she stayed in bed a good thirty minutes, musing the possibilities, before putting bare feet to cold floor and fully opening her eyes.

Perhaps it was a combination, she decided after she'd showered and dressed. Having Juliette working with her for longer than a two-hour stretch would certainly be a novelty. And Sylvie had spent so much of her time during the past two months in taking care of details that an evening out was very appealing. Of course, she hadn't allowed Juliette's business to occupy her every waking moment—or rather Max hadn't allowed her to do so.

He'd teased her relentlessly on some days, made

her angry on others, but his entire purpose in life seemed to be getting her away from Hannah Lee House. Not that he always succeeded, but he tried daily nonetheless. Persuading her to take a walk, a drive, a hike, a rest, or some other form of activity was the type of casual bantering he appeared to enjoy the most. Some days he'd worked right beside her doing whatever needed to be done, and other days he'd simply observed; Sylvie, preferring to call a spade a spade, told him flatly on those occasions to find some other place to loiter.

There had been days, though, when she hadn't seen him at all, and despite her better judgment, she had recognized a feeling—albeit small—of disappointment. Max kept her going. Sylvie had realized that over the Thanksgiving holiday. He kept her entertained and he kept her intermittently irritated, half the time with him and half the time with her sister. He fueled the resentment she felt toward Juliette's inability to make and carry out a decision, and yet Sylvie felt obligated to defend Juliette against Max's if-she-can't-swim-she-ought-to-get-out-of-the-water philosophy.

It wasn't always easy. In fact, Juliette made it increasingly more difficult. Benton was either unaware of the responsibilities that she was letting slide or unable to see any fault in her at all. Which was understandable. Juliette certainly could find no fault with him.

When she was at the dress shop, she was given to long, daydreaming silences or glowing accounts of Benton Prestridge's wise and witty sayings. Max offered a few wise sayings of his own, which Juliette accepted with an unoffended smile and Sylvie wished he had kept for his own, but nothing could dent Juliette's happiness. Even Sylvie had occasionally caught herself humming the same ridiculous love songs she heard her sister singing. It was late Saturday afternoon before it occurred to Sylvie that there might be a connection between the melodies she hummed and Max.

"Where's Max?" Juliette walked into the room with a can of soda in her hand and sank onto the bottom step.

Sylvie brushed the back of her hand across her forehead and critically eyed the baseboard she'd been painting. "I don't know. I haven't seen him all day. Why?"

"No reason. From the kitchen it sounded like you were humming, and you usually only do that if he's here."

"Don't be ridiculous, Juliette." Sylvie put down the paintbrush as her gaze continued checking for streaks.

"Well, it's true."

With an exasperated sigh Sylvie turned on her heel. "I don't sing, and I almost never hum."

"You don't have to pretend with me, Sylvie Anne. *I* heard you just now, and I've heard you a lot of other times, too, always when Max was here. Except for just now. But I'll bet you were thinking of him, weren't you?"

Frowning, Sylvie eyed her sister with caution. Juliette sounded agitated and looked somewhat annoyed. If Sylvie were any judge, there was an underlying reason for the conversation that had nothing to do with humming. "Is something bothering you, Julie?"

"Why would you think that? There's nothing wrong with me. I'm just impatient to be finished with this house." A momentary guilt flickered across her face. "With the repairs and stuff, I mean. You know I can't wait to open up shop and become the proprietress of Hannah Lee House Habiliments."

That was a possible explanation. Juliette always preferred to skip straight from the idea to the congratulations at the end.

"I know how anxious you are," Sylvie said dryly. "Maybe if you'd spend a little more time here working on—"

"You sound just like Benton! Lately he's been . . . Well, if that's the way you want to be, fine. But I'm going home." Juliette stood, a portrait of aggrieved innocence. "I thought *you* would understand, Sylvie Anne."

Which was a pretty tall order, Sylvie thought, given the circumstances. Still, she was beginning to gain a fairly good assessment of Juliette's problem. "I can't believe Benton has been giving you a hard time about your business. He seems content with the way you're juggling work and . . . other activities."

Juliette sucked in her lower lip. "He ought to be happy. I'm doing the best I can."

Sylvie straightened. "Are you and Benton having a small disagreement?"

"Now who's being ridiculous?" Juliette returned to the defensive and Sylvie felt a brief sadness. Once Juliette would have confided everything at the first hint of sisterly sympathy. "Benton and I are fine. Just fine. You'll see tonight. We're going with you and Max on the candlelight tour and we have tickets to the play too."

"Oh," Sylvie said. "That will be fun."

"Yes. Well, I'm leaving now. Why don't you put that paint away for today? You might as well—"

"I've just got a bit more to go and the baseboard will be done."

Juliette tapped her foot, then shrugged. "I'll get my purse and go on home." She started toward the kitchen, but stopped halfway out of the room. "Oh, Sylvie, may I borrow your key? I forgot mine this morning."

"It's in the zippered pocket of my billfold." Sylvie again turned her attention to the baseboard, but she caught herself, and Juliette, in time. "Don't forget to leave the door unlocked and the key on the table at home, Juliette." She paused to consider the effect of her reminder. "Promise you won't forget."

Julie lifted her hand to emphasize her sincerity. "I won't forget."

Stifling a niggling doubt, Sylvie signaled her appreciation with a smile and returned her attention to painting. She heard Juliette leave, but didn't look up from her task. As the brush glided soundlessly over the newly sanded wood, her thoughts drifted into fuzzy focus.

Humming? A frown of concentration followed the even strokes of the paintbrush. Of course, she knew she had been guilty earlier in the afternoon, and she remembered once, or maybe twice, before . . . typically.

But because of Max? What a ridiculous, typical Juliette idea. Sylvie shook her head and let a wry smile lift the corners of her mouth.

Humming! Of all things.

In the darkened theater, just as Scrooge was confronted by the eerie and silent Ghost of Christmas Yet to Come, Max reached for Sylvie's hand. Her heart jumped and she gave him a suspicious look, but he didn't appear to be unnerved by the apocalyptic specter. Surely he didn't think she was frightened by a character in a story she, and probably everyone else in the audience, knew by memory?

He glanced at her, smiled, and looked back at the stage. She wiggled her fingers slightly, but didn't withdraw her hand from his warm, cradling touch. It was pleasant and oddly sensual to sit in the dark holding hands with Max. As pleasant as the entire evening had been so far. The Candlelight Tour had been a leisurely, enjoyable excursion through a few businesses and homes decorated for the season with handmade ornaments and trimmings. The play was good and . . .

Her eyes followed the strong angle of his jawline to trace the character lines at the corner of his mouth. Max smiled more than any man she'd ever met. And he laughed often, not with the enigmatic, mocking sort of amusement so many men displayed, but with genuine pleasure. Max was one of the few people she knew who were comfortable enough with themselves to be natural with others. From the casual, overlong style of his dark hair to the well-worn, but obviously comfortable, tennis shoes he so often wore, Max made no effort to conform to her very definite ideas about life and life-styles. At first that had annoyed her, but lately she hardly even thought about it. Max was . . . Max: her friend, her adversary, and sometimes her ally.

When he glanced at her again, she realized she'd

regard made her think he recognized the evasive action for what it was: uncertainty.

Applause signaled a welcome diversion and the end of the play. In the aftermath of curtain calls there were the slow, rumbling sounds of an audience returning to separate conversations and individual plans. Sylvie stood and reached for her coat, but Max was already lifting it to her shoulders. As he pulled it around her, his eyes caught hers and held her motionless. Slowly, sensually, his smile unfolded, melting the edges of her uncertainty.

What if the seductive, off-again, on-again game he'd been playing all week wasn't a game at all? she wondered. Sylvie tucked the possibility out of sight and returned his smile in the most casual manner she could manage.

"For a town that gets very quiet after the tourist season, this seems to be a pretty noisy place."

It was a moment before Max relinquished her gaze or her shoulders. "In the past couple of years there's been a real effort to extend the season into December. I suppose Eureka Springs eventually could become a year-round attraction."

"You don't sound enthusiastic about the idea."

He stepped into the aisle and waited for her. With a touch of his hand at the small of her back, they began the slow progress to the exit. "Too much work. And you know how I feel about that."

"Keeping your nose to the grindstone results in a sore nose," Sylvie said dryly. "Isn't that your philosophy?"

He increased the pressure of his hand, urging her to keep moving. "I'll admit I'm partial to my nose the way it is."

"It's a good thing all the shopkeepers don't share your opinion."

"For your information I happen to know several people in town who like my nose every bit as much as I do."

She rewarded his nonsense with a smile. "Sorry, Max, I had no idea that was a 'sore' spot."

This time he smiled, but his accompanying chuckle was lost in the shuffle as the person next to Sylvie knocked her against Max's side. His arm went around her and pulled her close, guiding and protecting her until they reached the foyer of the auditorium. Once there, Max stopped to button his coat and Sylvie felt a pang of disappointment that she was no longer in need of his sheltering arm.

She caught the feeling and bundled it away as a passing fancy. Pulling on her hat, she followed Max to the entrance doors. Outside, the air was cold and bracing, with intermittent snowflakes that floated into sight and vanished on contact. Sylvie didn't know why she felt as if the evening had just been touched by magic, but as she walked beside Max and the crowd thinned to scattered groups of people, magic seemed an acceptable explanation for her contentment.

"Did you enjoy the play?" Max asked.

"Very much. Did you?"

"Yes, especially the last part"—his smile whispered with secrets—"when you held my hand."

Sylvie decided not to argue over who held whose hand. "I thought perhaps you were frightened by the ghosts and in need of a reassuring touch."

"Thank you," he said. "I'm still a bit shaky. Would you mind?"

With a laugh she took her hand from her coat pocket and tucked it inside Max's fleece-lined pocket alongside his hand. His fingers closed over hers and warmth rippled through her, like the anticipation of a fire on a winter morning. "Who reassured you during the play last year, Max?"

"I didn't go. The Attic was one of the stores on the Candlelight Tour last year, and Miriam and I were too busy with that."

"Really? You didn't mention that before."

"I didn't?"

"No." She cocked her head to regard him with sly suspicion. "You probably didn't want me to get the idea that you actually work on occasion."

"I don't know where you got the idea that I don't." His voice contained an edge of seriousness, but Sylvie squeezed his hand in teasing reply.

"Oh, it probably has something to do with the amount of time you spend supervising *my* work and trying to persuade me to play hooky for an afternoon."

"Do you consider that a waste of time?"

She paused. "Of course not, but it can't leave you much opportunity for your own work. I know this is the off-season and that The Attic is closed, but I thought you probably used the winter months to make the toys and dolls for the shop."

"It all gets done eventually. No one wins a Pulitzer Prize for being the first store owner in town to have the shelves restocked."

"Oh, I see your point. If I were you, I'd hold out for an Academy Award. More television coverage."

He gave her fingers a scolding pinch for being facetious. "And that would impress you, I suppose."

"Are you kidding? That would impress everyone!"

"Well, frankly, I believe I should hold out for a more coveted prize."

"Like what?"

"You, for example."

"For example? That's a backhanded sort of compliment, Max."

"I thought it was pretty straightforward."

"Which just shows how out of practice you are."

"I must be," he acknowledged somberly. "You never take anything I say seriously."

Sylvie laughed softly. "And what would you do, Max, if I did?"

His steps slowed, his lips tipped reluctantly upward, and inside the fleecy pocket his thumb caressed her hand in smooth circles. "I'd probably kiss you."

"And then what?"

"I'd be happy to show you."

Her heart stopped for a second, but she kept walking. It was pretty hard to misinterpret that kind of remark, but she thought perhaps she ought to give it a try. "Well, for now, you can show me a cup of coffee, since we're almost on your doorstep."

"And later?" Max asked in a low, suggestive tone.

"Later," Sylvie answered, matching him with a sultry tone of her own, "you can show me the workroom where you create all those wonderful toys."

Max sighed and remained silent until they reached the concrete steps in front of his house. Then he released her hand and gestured grandly toward the porch. "What a romantic way to end an evening. Almost as good as a crossword puzzle."

Sylvie laughed and led the way to the door, where

she waited while Max opened it, switched on a light, and motioned for her to enter. Inside, Max took her coat and casually tossed it on the couch.

"Come along," he said, moving toward the kitchen doorway. "You can tour the workroom to your heart's content while I prepare our nightcap."

"I'd prefer coffee." She dropped her hat onto the couch beside her coat and smoothed her disheveled hair.

Max stopped and shook his head. "Have you suddenly decided to take every word I say literally? I was referring to the coffee, Sylvie. Nightcap—coffee. Any other questions?"

She merely smiled and followed him into the kitchen, which was remarkably similar to Juliette's. Max stepped to another doorway, reached around the jamb, and flipped on a light. "Be my guest."

Sylvie didn't wait for further invitation. She'd wanted to see his studio for quite some time. In fact, she'd teased him for weeks, telling him she knew his workshop at home was a smoke screen, invented as an alibi for staying at home instead of going to his store.

But it was real. And so were the toys, in various stages of creation, that littered all the available work space. Max obviously *did* work here, and as she wandered at random about the room, Sylvie felt as if she were seeing a whole new facet in his personality.

The pride he took in his craft was evident in everything she saw. It still amazed her that Max's large hands could create the delicate, lifelike features of a doll's face. But there was something more here, an aura different from that of the toy store, a lingering sense of ideas rather than polished products. This room held a part of Max's soul, and Sylvie felt honored to have been allowed to enter it.

When she realized he was still standing in the doorway, she pivoted slowly, wanting to express her approval, but not knowing exactly how to go about it. "You could have invited me sooner. I'd never steal your secrets."

"Maybe I thought you'd steal something else."

She smiled gently, uncertain of his mood. "Don't worry. Your coffee recipe is safe with me."

His lips made no attempt to form an answering curve, and as he turned toward the kitchen, Sylvie called out to him. "Max? I was only—I just wondered why you never let me see your workroom before."

He turned back, his eyes dark and intensely blue, his expression pensive as he regarded her from the doorway. "A lot of *me* is in this room, Sylvie. Not everyone could understand that." He paused. "Maybe you don't either."

How could she not understand? She'd known for quite some time that he was a creative, tender, and sensitive man, she just hadn't realized how much she liked knowing it.

"I've never met anyone like you, Max." It wasn't what she wanted to say, but it was as close as she could come at the moment. "You must be a limited edition."

He stood there in the doorway, his eyes holding her steady, and then slowly, inexorably, she was drawn forward. Sylvie stopped just short of his reach, but as his hand grasped hers, she knew she'd somehow miscalculated. His arms went around her and her reaction was self-protective and involuntary.

"Have you tried to find a distributor for your dolls,

Max? I'm sure with the right marketing techniques, you could—"

"Not now, Sylvie." The remaining distance into his arms was bridged forcefully and without hesitation. Max took her lips roughly, but he excused his action with the knowledge that at least she would know he was serious.

Why did she always do that to him? Just when he felt she was beginning to understand, just when he'd decide she had finally accepted him as he was, she'd suggest something he needed to do in order to make himself better. She'd patronized him just now with her business expertise. Why did he allow her to act as if he were totally innocent of the most simple business logic and needed her guidance? Why did he . . .

The tension in her body ebbed beneath his touch, and the denigrating questions washed away with it. Max reacted instinctively, gathering her close, feeling her pliant response to his kiss. He discovered he no longer cared about anything except holding and touching her. Sylvie, finally, was returning his investment. Her lips moved against his, her body pressed into him, and he ached to hold her even closer. He'd thought from the first day they met that she was vulnerable beneath her veneer of brash sophistication; he'd known that, if she ever stopped thinking of him as a man who was not at all her type, she would discover the multitude of things they had in common.

But even as he savored the warm taste of her lips, he was aware of his own conflict. He wanted to make love to her, but how could he, when he knew she didn't understand his most basic motivations? Sylvie wanted him to be something he wasn't, something he would never be—not by her definition, anyway. Slowly, reluctantly, he drew back and watched the expression in her green eyes change from soft surrender to apprehensive questioning. His body told him to settle for the moment and strive to win her understanding later, but his heart warned him to hold out for more.

"If I'd known how impressed you'd be, I'd have invited you to my studio sooner."

Sylvie tried to catch her breath and her racing pulse. He sounded so unaffected, so *normal*. How could he be so nonchalant about a kiss that had changed her whole concept of the term *serious?* She drew a long, unsteady breath. "It's just as well you didn't."

"Why?" His voice was light, not teasing, but hardly shaky either.

With forefinger and thumb on either side of her glasses, she refocused, tried to find some logical answer, and finally said the first thing that came to mind. "I have no idea. I don't even know what I meant to say."

His grin was slow as he tapped her chin with a playful knuckle. "Take your time, Sylvie Anne. Maybe it will come to you." He turned and went into the kitchen, glancing back at her over his shoulder. "Ready for that nightcap now?"

Sylvie felt as if she'd just had one nightcap too many. "No." She followed him at a slower pace. "I probably should go home. If Juliette had car trouble or Benton trouble or anything, she might try to call. And since I'm here . . ." The sentence was lost along with her train of thought. Maybe she ought to have a nightcap after all, or another kiss. Or maybe she just ought to get the hell out of Max's kitchen.

"Since you're here?" Max prompted.

"No one's there. To answer the phone, I mean."

His eyes teased her again, and yet she recognized a shadowy tension at the corners of his mouth.

"Then I suppose you should be there. We can have coffee some other time."

He could have sounded a little unhappy about it, Sylvie thought. But Max wasn't the type to waste time on regrets. She didn't either. "Yes, some other time. I enjoyed the play and the tour. It was lovely, Max. Thank you."

"You're welcome. I'd offer to hold your hand while you walk across the yard, but I know you don't need that kind of protection. Good night, Sylvie. Be sure the door closes behind you. Sometimes the latch doesn't catch."

Put like that, she had little choice but to get her coat and hat from the living room and leave. If he didn't have the common courtesy to see her to the door, Sylvie decided he certainly didn't deserve a good-bye from her.

Outside, the snow welcomed her into a cold world that was turning whiter by the minute. Snowflakes waltzed past like debutantes at a winter ball. Sylvie stuck her hands in her coat pockets and lowered her head to keep the icy drops from her face. The white, frosty air made her think of the sugar angel in the candy-shop window. Only, of course, it was really crochet. . . .

Max had a lot to answer for, she decided. Kissing her like that and then sending her home alone. Juliette would have known how to turn that one kiss into several and win an overnight invitation if she'd wanted one. But Sylvie had gone straight from a promising beginning to a terse good-night and she didn't have any idea how it had happened. Actually, it was Max's fault. She had thought he was serious this time. All week long he'd smiled at her in that special way, touched her as if he couldn't help himself, watched her lips when she talked . . . little details that he'd meant for her to think about and wonder about and anticipate.

And she had, although she'd tempered the reasoning with a healthy measure of doubt. All her life she'd known the appropriate thing to say at all the appropriate moments . . . except when there was a man involved. She'd always had trouble adjusting from casual conversation, with which she was comfortable, to the whispered vows of undying devotion, with which she was distinctly uncomfortable. At the crucial moment in a relationship, when it was balanced precariously near commitment, she found herself skeptical, wondering if forever after was possible or just an advertising gimmick.

But Max had courted her in such a subtle, teasing sort of way that she hadn't considered the possibility of a relationship developing between them. And yet, tonight, she had believed he was serious. She'd *wanted* to believe it, and that in itself, she supposed, was the classic punch line to her own private joke. She, Sylvie Anne Smith, who would be thirty years old in a matter of weeks, who was ambitious and successful and particular, was serious about a man who was thirty-five and had no higher aim in life than to create exquisite toys that he was content to sell to tourists. He wore denim, flannel, and canvas almost exclusively, but when he kissed her, she didn't care if he *owned* a pinstripe suit.

Sylvie sighed her frustration with Max's behavior and with her own feelings. Well, she'd been warned. But who would have thought Juliette knew anything about fate?

When she reached the driveway, she paused. Her leased car was parked in the drive as usual, and Benton's sporty Datsun was parked closer to the house with Juliette's MG squeezed between the two. Sylvie pursed her lips and moved past the cars to the house.

The windows were dark and the only sign of habitation was the faraway sound of the stereo. A little mood music. Hardly *Bolero*, Sylvie thought, but close enough. She wished Juliette had switched on the porch light, but in a very few minutes Sylvie realized that was the least of her troubles.

She was locked out. The front door, the back door, and the windows were locked, and Juliette had the keys, all of them. With a sigh Sylvie looked around. Pounding on the door was a possible means of entry, she supposed, but considering the evidence— Benton's car, the stereo, and no lights—Sylvie decided that would be wasted effort for some time to come.

Her gaze slid to the lighted porch next door as she considered her options. A plan of action wasn't difficult to decide; she would tell Max she'd changed her mind about the nightcap and first thing Monday morning she would see an attorney about putting Juliette up for adoption.

CHAPTER EIGHT

"What do I get out of this?" Max asked as he watched Sylvie take off her coat and toss it on the sofa.

"Backgammon," she replied with crisp, clear irritation. "Double or nothing."

"Hey, I didn't lock you out. Keep in mind that I'm the rescuer in this situation. I've offered you the use of my phone or my couch. What more could a rescuee ask for?"

"A little mood music." The words snapped past her lips with all the frustration of the last half hour.

"Sorry. The closest I could come to your mood is a recording of the *1812 Overture*."

"How do you feel about humming?"

"Well, I prefer a full orchestra, but if you want to—"

"Forget it, Max." Sylvie ran restless fingers through her hair. "Would it be possible to have that nightcap now? Something lighter, brighter, and more numbing than coffee?"

He folded his arms across his chest and regarded her pensively. "Wine?"

"That ought to do it." She sank onto the sofa and leaned down to rub the chill from her ankles. Her feet were cold, too, but as she cupped the back of her shoe to remove it, she glanced at Max. He was still standing, still eyeing her with undue caution. "Do you mind if I take off my shoes?"

The corner of his mouth twitched ever so slightly, before mischief etched the crease in his cheek. "Feel free to take off anything you like."

"What is this? I ask for a glass of wine and you suddenly become Mr. Hospitality?" She kept her gaze on him as she slid off first one gray pump and then the other.

"Just trying to be a good neighbor."

"Oh, is that why you practically pushed me out the door a little while ago?" She hadn't meant to mention that, hadn't wanted him to know it bothered her, but at the moment she couldn't think of a good reason for him not to know. Consequently, her tone was sharp and brusque. "You might have walked with me as far as the front door, Max."

"I wasn't feeling very neighborly then." His amusement faded from sight. "And come to think of it, I don't feel very neighborly now either. Your quarrel isn't with me, Sylvie Anne, so . . . ." He seemed to think better of completing the sentence and walked past her, stopping in the kitchen doorway to look back. "How much wine do you think it will take?"

Sylvie lifted her chin. "To do what?"

"To lighten, brighten, or numb you." Max raised his brows in answer to the challenge in her voice. "Of course."

"Of course," she said sweetly. Rising, she followed him into the kitchen and watched as he opened a cabinet. "How much will it take to make you feel neighborly?"

"I don't know, but we're not going to find out to-night."

"Does that mean I'm drinking alone?"

He set a glass on the counter and opened the refrigerator. "You got it, neighbor."

Sylvie pursed her lips, pushed up her glasses, and tucked a strand of hair behind her ear. She waited until he set the wine bottle on the table and uncorked it. "I've changed my mind, Max. I'm not thirsty after all."

His eyes clashed with hers across the width of the kitchen; then he shrugged, recorked the bottle, and put it back in the refrigerator. Just as he put away the crystal glass and closed the cabinet door, Sylvie cleared her throat.

"On second thought . . . ."

"Think again, Sylvie. It's cold outside." The slant of his lips left her in no doubt that he was only partially teasing.

"It's cold in here." She leaned a shoulder against the door casing. "But I can't figure out why. *I'm* the one who's locked out. *I'm* the one who's being taken advantage of."

"Does that give you a monopoly on the feeling?" Max braced a hand on the counter and irritably tapped his fingers. "Has it ever occurred to you, Sylvie, that Juliette isn't the only member of your family who takes advantage?"

Sylvie drew a deep breath. "I assume you're not referring to my father."

"No one could fault your intelligence," Max said, "but your sensitivity is another matter."

"I don't have to listen to this." She pivoted away from his accusing blue eyes. "It's bad enough—"

"Which only proves my point."

She pivoted back. "It proves nothing. If I—"

"If you were the least bit sensitive to my feelings you wouldn't always be on the receiving end of this relationship. You'd—"

"What relationship?" She took a step toward him, stopped, touched her glasses, and let her hand fall to her side. "I didn't think we . . . It was never . . ."

"Well, what *did* you think, Sylvie? That I had nothing better to do with my time? Didn't you consider that maybe—just maybe—I *made* time to be with you? That I enjoy your company, that I like being with you? You've never even admitted that you like having me around. And it would be nice to hear you say it once in a while. It would be nice to have you tell me how you feel and what you want. A relationship has to be reciprocal, Sylvie. Don't you think it's about time you faced up to that?"

"I told you in the beginning I wasn't looking for a relationship, Max."

"And I said one just might find you anyway."

Her heart was beating so hard and so fast she could hardly think. "What did I say to that?"

Max rubbed his palm across his cheek. "I don't remember. What do you say now?"

"Is there an interpreter in the house?" He didn't smile. Neither did she. "I don't know what you want me to say, Max. You've accused me of being insensitive and taking advantage of you, but I"—she paused, looked away from his penetrating gaze, then met his eyes again—"I'm not good at relationships, Max. This sort of thing makes me uncomfortable."

"Look, I'm the same guy who beats you at backgammon. I'm the one who helps you hang wallpaper.

I'm the one who points out your mistakes to you, remember? How can you be uncomfortable with me, Sylvie Anne?"

She moistened her lips. Couldn't he hear the revealing thud of her heartbeat? "Because I can't tell when you're serious and when you're not."

"Shall I tell you?"

"No!" She swallowed the panicky feeling in her throat. "No, I'm sure it would lose something in the translation."

Max crossed his arms on his chest and regarded the floor for the space of two deep breaths and a sigh. "What do you want, Sylvie? From a relationship? From me?"

She just wanted him, but she could hardly say that. He seemed to want discussion, the whys and wherefores. She wanted something more . . . memorable. The whole thing was ridiculous, anyway.

"I don't know, Max. What does it matter?" She turned and walked into the living room with the half-formed intention of phoning Juliette and Benton, regardless of the circumstances.

Max shattered that idea with the touch of his hands on her shoulders. And in that moment she knew it did matter. She knew *she* mattered. He hadn't let her walk away this time. He was pulling her back against him, willing her to relax.

"Sylvie." It was the softest of whispers and it floated all the way to her fingertips on a sigh. His hand lifted her hair and a feathery breath warmed the back of her neck, just before she felt the touch of his lips. "You seem shorter," he said against her skin.

"No . . . shoes." She thought she sounded rather casual, despite the ripple of tension closing in on her vocal cords. But apparently Max was unimpressed by her tone of voice. He kept teasing her with tiny, barely-there kisses, from her nape to just below her earlobe and back again to her nape.

"Really, Max," she murmured. "This isn't . . . necessary."

"Oh, but it is, Sylvie." His lips found the hiding place of a dozen delicate shivers and sent them cascading through her senses like a shower of rainbows. "It is."

He placed one hand at her waist and his other hand kneaded her shoulder with soft intent. Sylvie wondered if she ought to make some form of protest, but she hesitated to do so. What if he believed she meant it? No, she'd waited too long for this . . . although she hadn't realized *this* was what she'd been waiting for. Arching her neck to give him free access, she closed her eyes and savored the warm support of his arms, the disastrous incoherence of her logic.

She had to form his name twice on her lips before it became an audible murmur. "Max?"

"Mmmm?"

"You're . . . serious now." It sounded more like a question than a statement, but Max was in no hurry to answer either way. In slow, rhythmic circles his fingers caressed the silky dress fabric that covered her stomach, and his breath felt immeasurably tantalizing wherever it touched her skin.

"Not yet, but I'm getting there," he said, and for countless imaginable reasons heat rushed to every nerve ending in her body.

She made a quarter turn, allowing her hands to explore the rough, muscled texture of his arm, allowing him to explore new territory along her throat. "You're not teasing, are you?"

"Do you always ask so many questions?"

"Only when someone is trying to take advantage of me."

The nibbling kisses stopped and Max turned her to face him. Her breasts ached to feel the sensual rub of his chest and her hands went to his shoulders of their own accord. Sylvie blinked in an effort to clear her head, but the expression in his eyes took everything out of focus again.

"Is that what you think, Sylvie? That I'm trying to take advantage of you?"

Her lips curved with the growing need to taste his. "I hope you'll do more than try, Max. Fair's fair, and since I—"

He took the rest of the words along with her mouth and Sylvie melted against him. An odd sensation, she thought, melting like that. She'd always supposed it was a descriptive phrase, but now she knew better. Her thighs, her hips, her breasts, her whole body seemed suddenly to blend into his large and angular symmetry. And his lips. God, she'd never before been a part of such possessive intimacy, such unarguable promise.

Her hands slid beneath his shirt collar and her fingers tangled in the dark tendrils of hair at his nape. The scent of snow and cold air still filled her senses, but she didn't know if it clung to Max or was simply a part of the private world they had shared all evening. She should have known this would happen, should have recognized that in his arms was the one place she longed to be. It had happened often throughout her life; what she ultimately wanted turned out to be the thing she'd most denied wanting. And she'd denied wanting Max. He had been right. She'd hardly even admitted liking him, and she'd certainly never entertained thoughts of a relationship.

But here it was, full-grown and aching to be acknowledged. With a deeply satisfying sigh Sylvie parted her lips in concession and moved her hands until her thumbs could stroke the firm line of his jaw. When he released her and started to pull away, she cupped his face with her palms, keeping him close enough for an instant replay.

"You constantly surprise me, Max."

"I know." He brushed a kiss on the corner of her mouth. "When are you going to stop being surprised and start being impressed?"

"Oh, I don't know. Probably about the same time you take off your shoes."

"That soon, huh?"

She brought temptation to his lips with a touch of her finger. "All talk and no action makes me uncomfor—" A stockinged foot rubbed across her toe and Sylvie glanced down. "How did you do that so fast?"

His smile was lazily sensual. "Never underestimate a man who wears loafers."

"How do you feel about girls who wear glasses?"

"Girls?" One hand slid from her waist to trace the curve of her hip, adding unnecessary emphasis to his opinion that she could hardly be classified as a girl. "I have no idea. But I made the mistake of underestimating you—a woman who wears glasses—and you see how that's ended."

"Well, actually, Max, I didn't even see how it started." She dropped her gaze to the placket of his shirt and let her finger follow at a slower pace. "Do you think you could . . . demonstrate?"

He cupped her chin and raised her eyes to his. "With pleasure."

A smooth expectancy drifted through her, enhanced by the thudding heartbeat she could feel beneath her palm, amplified by the sudden urgency in his kiss. When Max bent to lift her into his arms, Sylvie released her breath in a rush, as if that would make her lighter, easier for him to carry. But he didn't seem to expend any great effort in lifting her, and by the time they reached the shadowy bedroom, she was far more breathless than he.

Max stopped beside the bed and shifted his supporting arms. Sylvie kept her hands on his shoulders, her lips opened to his, and let her body slide the length of his. Her dress anchored around her waist, leaving her legs bare except for the nylon hose. The textured wool of Max's trousers tickled her skin and the hardness of his thigh taunted her. Her breasts protested the restraints of clothing with an aching fullness that was not satisfied by a distant touch.

But Max would not be hurried. His pulse thrummed with desire, a sweet, wildly reverent desire, to possess her. His caresses were hungry but deliberate, urgent but controlled. Her nearness, the fragrance and feel of her in his arms, her very willingness, made it difficult but imperative to take time. Sylvie needed a slow hand, he'd known that all along. He'd won her acceptance and her trust by degrees; he would win her body the same way.

He drew back, hesitant to rush even so much as a button until he was certain of his own ability to move without haste, to take things step by easy step. His lips curved as he looked at her, observing the rich creamy color of her skin and the moist, rose-tinted outline of her lips. He didn't think he'd ever before seen her hair so attractively disheveled. He had wondered often how it would look after he'd loved her, its red-gold fire splayed across his pillow. Now he would know. Now . . .

No. He shouldn't think of that yet. The tension was wrapping itself around him, tugging at his reason as the soft hint of doubt in her sea-green eyes tugged at his heart. Sylvie, ever confident, always self-assured, was trembling in his arms. He didn't believe she was even aware of it, but he felt it and knew her doubt was for her own ability to respond, to please. As his hand touched her cheek in reassurance, the need for tenderness became paramount in his mind.

He took the frame of her glasses between his fingers, wanting to remove the symbol of sophistication. "Do you need these?" he asked quietly.

"Only if you want me to see."

"Don't you know braille?"

"I'm nearsighted, Max. Not blind."

He lifted the glasses from her face and set them on the bedside table. "Then I'll be careful to stay close. Very, very close."

A purring consent vibrated in her throat, and then her arms were pulling him closer, her lips were seeking his, her tongue was issuing invitations he simply couldn't refuse. Desire ricocheted into heady and wondrous sensations and Max let it build to a strong and steady demand. By turns he stroked her with passion and then soothed her with a gentling massage. Her dress was unneeded and distracting and was soon discarded along with his shirt.

He delighted in the play of shadows across her satiny skin. His fingertip traced the moon-laced patterns from her shoulder all the way to the tiny flower appliqué between her breasts, but he grew impatient and unhooked the bra to cup her warm flesh in his palm. She was silken to the touch and conformed to the fit of his hand as easily as porcelain slip conformed to the mold. But Max knew, as he lowered his mouth to her breast, that he wouldn't want Sylvie Anne to conform in any way. She wasn't his to shape and sculpt, to mold into some subjective design. She was his, for the moment, to please and to find pleasure in, to give to and to take from. He wanted her surrender and knew the price would be more than he'd bargained for, but he also knew it was worth the cost.

Sylvie melted a little deeper into his embrace when his tongue circled and teased her breast. She was absorbing the riotous sensations he created, the rough-soft texture of his bare chest and shoulders. She hadn't realized how good his touch could be, how right Max would feel in her arms. It was astonishing, really, to be taken by surprise like this. He'd always treated her gently, but now he caressed her as if she were as fragile as porcelain and as valuable as a Ming vase. No one before had ever touched her with such tender devotion to detail. No one before had ever made her feel quite so special. And no one before had ever evoked such dramatic and passionate emotions in her.

She wanted Max, needed him with an intensity she usually reserved for debates about vital issues. But Max had somehow become vital to her well-being. He had somehow become as necessary to her as the air she breathed, and her inner debate centered on when, not why. Why didn't matter. In fact, nothing seemed to matter except getting Max to release her long enough to shed all semblance of clothing and inhibitions, just long enough to pull him onto the bed with her.

It took time, Sylvie discovered, but she accomplished the goal and finally Max was lying naked beside her, exploring every curve and secret of her body just as she was exploring him. Their lips met, clung, and trailed fiery kisses as each sought new territory, new vistas of pleasure. But when Max reached the uncharted smoothness of her stomach, he lingered only long enough to claim it for his own before returning again to her lips, and Sylvie found she was dissatisfied to be too long without the sustenance of his kiss.

A wild desire banked, flared, and burned itself into emotions Sylvie didn't recognize. Her heart pounded madly, subsided to an uneven, but easier, rhythm, then raced like a Thoroughbred fresh out of the gate. And when, at last, Max moved to fulfill the promise of building passions, she knew she'd been touched by his magic. Nothing in her life would ever again be quite the same. And oddly, Sylvie knew she would be content and comfortable with this new relationship.

Her hands tracked the muscular ridges of his back and settled on the lean slope of his hips. There she could encourage him, guide him through the maze of wondrous sensations that were even now chasing through her veins. Her eyes closed with the sweet pain of surrender and then she moved against him, arching her body to his, accepting, stroking, and releasing him, only to repeat the seduction again and again and again.

"Sylvie," he whispered with the hoarse, throaty sound of intense pleasure . . . or pain . . . or both. Pressing her lips to his, she met the thrust of his tongue and a rush of untamed needs whipped and whirled inside her, rising and spiraling and finally exploding in splendor.

There *was* magic in the world, she realized as passion ebbed and drifted into sweet languor. Max had shown her. He had shared it with her. She'd never expected to experience a grand and glorious passion; she'd certainly never suspected she might experience it with Max.

Luckily, she thought in drowsy contentment, fate had listened to her heart, not the thousand and one reasons given by her practical nature.

In the cool, silvery light of morning Sylvie made her way to the kitchen and as quietly as possible started the coffee brewing. The aroma soon trickled through her hazy thoughts, awakening memories of the night before. With the softest smile her lips had ever known, she walked to the window and looked out. From this vantage point she could see little more than rooftops and eaves of the town below. Eureka Springs was nestled into the Ozark hills, a patchwork of Victorian color on a field of white. Only a week into December and already winter had settled in. The snow sparkled everywhere, like fairy dust on a gingerbread village.

Fairy dust? Only one night with Max and already she was losing her ability to think rationally. Sylvie wrapped her arms across her chest, snuggled her hands into the folds of Max's flannel shirt, and turned away from the view. God, she felt wonderful. How had he done that?

A humming sigh eased past her lips as she hugged herself along with the remembrance of all that he had done. Her smile curved just for her own pleasure, and she wondered if being in love felt anything like this. If it did, then she'd spent far too much time on practice runs. Why hadn't Juliette told her what real loving was like?

Simple, she realized. Juliette didn't know. No one else could possibly know. She, Sylvie Anne, was the only woman in the world who felt this way. She was poised on the edge of discovery, almost, but not quite, in love. And he wasn't even her type. How amazing. How completely ridiculous. Maybe she was dreaming. Sylvie hugged herself a little tighter and walked toward the workshop. To be on the safe side, she decided she just wouldn't wake up.

She followed an impulse through the doorway and into Max's private room. His workshop, an important part of Max, and yet, it didn't seem to jibe with the man she knew. Or thought she knew. Of course she realized she knew little about his work, even less about its importance in his life. A major miscalculation on her part, she thought. She needed to know, wanted to learn, what was important to him and why. And examining the clues in his workshop was the first step toward finding that out.

She reached for a block of wood on the tabletop and lifted it in her hand. It was rough to the touch, but the grain ran smoothly beneath the penciled outline of a caboose. Max had sketched the design he intended to carve from the wood, and Sylvie traced her fingertip over the lines. Putting it on the table again, she moved on to look at the rest of the room, paying more attention to detail than she had last night. There were molds and packages, tools, brushes, and a large kiln in the corner, but she examined those in a glance, turning her whole attention to the display of dolls on a low shelf.

These were not like the dolls in the toy shop. She bent for a closer look. These were real-life figures, a man in the robes of royalty, a woman with long, flowing hair and medieval dress. King Arthur and Guinevere. Sylvie didn't know how she recognized them, yet it was clear whom the dolls were meant to represent. Maybe that was the skill Max brought to his creations, she thought, that ability to capture a fantasy and make it tangible.

She felt a little humbled by the realization that he was more than skilled at his craft. He was an artist in the truest sense of the word. She had been quick to dismiss his work as a hobby turned into a business, and not a particularly profitable business at that. She hadn't asked many questions, hadn't been terribly interested in his toys. Until now. Now she wanted to know everything about him. She wanted to be a part of his routine, as he was already a part of hers. Maybe she could help him—

What a dumb idea. Sylvie straightened both her posture and her smile. She would be of little use to Max in this workshop. Her skills lay more in the area of business and organization. Now, if he ever decided to market his toys . . . The possibility loomed into focus. Of course, why hadn't she thought of it immediately? Max had a gold mine in this one little room. All he needed was a connection with the world of marketing and distribution. His dolls could be selling in stores throughout the country, and selling well.

Sylvie shook her head at the potential of her idea. It was conceivable that Max could become tremendously successful. No, she thought, it was a foregone conclusion. And more than that, she could do something to help, something to prove she wasn't insensitive to his feelings.

But what was he going to say? She considered that as she roamed restlessly about the room and decided he would give her a resounding no. Hadn't he told her that not everyone could understand the way he felt about his work? Hadn't he questioned whether or not *she* understood? She had wondered why he spoke so casually of his work, but now that she saw how serious he was about it, she realized he felt insecure in his talent. That, undoubtedly, was the reason he hadn't tried to find a distributor before.

Before. Sylvie hesitated to accept the idea already formed and waiting in her mind. Max would probably strangle her. But she could make success happen for him, or at least give him a push in the right direction. She knew she could. It would be as simple as contacting a few people. She wouldn't make any commitments, just inquiries. And once she received a positive response . . . well, then Max could take over from there. Why not?

The more she thought about it, the more appealing the idea became. There was no risk involved this way. Max didn't have to know until it was an accomplished fact. Perfect, Sylvie decided, from every angle. She'd begin checking into the possible markets tomorrow. It shouldn't take too long. Maybe she would have a wonderful Christmas present for him.

Returning to the kitchen, she eyed the freshly made coffee with disdain. Who needed caffeine? She would slip back into bed and allow Max to awaken her. A perfectly delightful idea, she told herself as she stifled a yawn. The second-best idea of the morning.

The soft smile regained strength with the anticipation of Max's embrace. Forget second best, she thought. If she was going to fall heart over head in love—and she had no doubt that was exactly what she was about to do—she was going first class all the way.

CHAPTER NINE

"Well, I don't know why you're upset," Juliette said from the doorway of Sylvie's bedroom. *"I'm* not the one who stayed out all night."

Sylvie answered that bit of glaring illogic with a skeptical lift of her brows and then unequivocally pulled back the sheets of her bed. Placing her glasses on the bedside table, she hoped Juliette would take the hint and leave. A mood was a fragile thing and Sylvie really preferred to keep the one she had. Her sister, unfortunately, seemed to think it needed improvement.

"And not only that," Juliette continued, "you were gone all day too. My God, Sylvie, it isn't like you to come home from a Saturday-night date at nine o'clock on *Sunday* night." She shook her head in sad commentary. "And now you're going to bed."

"And to sleep," Sylvie said pointedly as she got into bed and tucked the covers around herself. She wished it were Max's bed, but she'd decided it would be best to return home and give them both some time. She didn't want to rush the discovery of where this new phase in their friendship—she still felt oddly hesitant about using the term relationship—might lead. And she didn't want Max to get the wrong idea.

One night, and one perfectly wonderful day, didn't mean she was ready to move in with him. Even if he'd asked her. Which he hadn't. "Would you mind turning out the light as you leave, Julie?"

"Sylvie!" It was a plaintive cry, full of accusation and sibling demand. "If you think for one minute . . . honestly, I can't believe you don't want to talk about this. You should never go to sleep when you're angry. Didn't you know that?"

"I'm not angry."

"Of course you are. But it really isn't my fault, you know." Juliette sank cross-legged onto the foot of the bed and Sylvie had little choice but to pull her feet out of the way. "I'm sorry I forgot about returning your key and I'm sorry I locked you out. But everything worked out for the best."

Only a fool would argue that line of indiscriminate reasoning, and Sylvie wasn't feeling particularly foolish or argumentative at the moment. Still, it was apparent that Juliette wasn't going to go away. She was intent upon apologizing or explaining or something equally distracting. With a sigh Sylvie pushed up, levering herself on an elbow as she propped the pillows against the headboard and leaned back against them. She debated putting on her glasses, but decided this was one time she preferred keeping her sister slightly out of focus. "All right, Juliette, let's have it."

"There, you see? You are upset."

For the sake of progress Sylvie decided she might as well take the offensive. "If I'm upset, Juliette, it's because you're twenty-two years old and you're still losing your keys, borrowing mine, and then locking me out of the house."

"You could have called."

"I could have yelled myself hoarse and you wouldn't have heard me."

Juliette gave an exaggerated sigh. "I meant you could have telephoned."

"I could have done a lot of things. All of them irrelevant to the subject we're discussing."

"Oh, I don't know." Juliette propped her elbows on her knees and her chin in her hands. "I think what you did do is pretty relevant."

Sylvie lifted her hands in frustration. "I spent the night at Max's house. Would you be happier if I'd slept on the porch?"

"You spent the night *with* Max. There's a difference, you know." Her gold brows arched suggestively. "So you see, if I hadn't locked you—"

"Juliette, how can you try to take credit for what happened last night?"

"And what did happen?"

Sylvie reached for her glasses and brought her sister's pert innocence into view. "We played backgammon. What did you and Benton do?"

"We got engaged."

"Engaged?" Sylvie leaned forward. "As in to be married?"

Juliette giggled, nodded, and giggled again. "Isn't that the most amazing thing you ever heard?"

Amazing wasn't the right word, but Sylvie laughed her agreement just the same. Her feelings at the moment were mixed, but she couldn't resist the bubbly excitement of Julie's happiness.

"Benton Prestridge is the luckiest lawyer in Arkansas. Maybe in all fifty states."

"Oh, no." Juliette's smile softened with a tender

seriousness. "I'm the lucky one. I mean, Benton is so . . ." Expression and tone of voice conveyed the message that Benton was wonderful beyond description and Sylvie, in a moment of sisterly understanding, nodded her complete accord.

"Yesterday," Juliette said, "well, really it was on Friday, Benton and I had a fight. Sort of a fight, anyway." She frowned, remembering. "Actually, it was a big fight. He thought I should be spending more time at Hannah Lee House and that I was letting you take all the responsibility and that I wasn't acting very mature about the whole business. Oh, he went on and on, Sylvie, saying I wasn't being fair to you or to me. After all, he said, it was my idea and I should be working on getting the restoration done but I was being irresponsible and leaving everything for you to do." Juliette tangled her fingers into the blond curls at her temple and then extended her hand in apology. "I'm sorry, Sylvie. I didn't mean to be unfair. I didn't think—Benton says that's one of my biggest problems—but really I didn't know . . ."

"It's all right." Sylvie didn't know where the reassurance came from, but she gave it unhesitatingly. She'd learned years before that frustration and forgiveness went hand in hand with being kin to Juliette. And it was nice to know there was someone else to tell Julie what Max had been telling Sylvie for weeks. "I suppose you resolved your differences with Benton last night and everything's all right now, since you're—God, Juliette, are you sure about getting married?"

"Yes."

The very simplicity of the answer was an affirmation in itself, and Sylvie smiled. "So, when do I have to give you a wedding present?"

"Valentine's Day." Juliette dimpled in anticipation. "But gifts will be accepted anytime before or after. And you'll wear red, of course."

"Of course." Sylvie shifted position and straightened the pillow at her back. "I would never wear any other color when giving you a wedding gift."

"At the wedding." Juliette aimed a swift and inaccurate kick at Sylvie's foot. "You'll be the maid of honor, Syl. And I'll throw the bouquet to you, but you have to promise to give it back."

"Oh, you have my word on that."

Juliette grinned and began tapping her fingers against her shin. She pursed her lips and let her gaze wander around the bedroom. Sylvie braced herself for a change of topic and guessed that the Hannah Lee was about to enter the conversation.

"You know"—Juliette broached the subject with caution—"I have to make a decision about Hannah Lee House." Wide blue eyes turned to Sylvie, seeking support. "Benton says I could commute from Fayetteville, but I don't think I'd like that very much. In fact, I think I'd hate it." When Sylvie made no comment, Juliette sighed. "I *know* I'd hate it. I'm going to sell the house. There's really nothing else to do."

It was a sensible decision, yet Sylvie felt a stab of disappointment just the same. She hated the idea that the dress shop wouldn't open. She'd wanted success for Juliette, but it was not to be. Not in business, anyway. And Sylvie accepted a share of the disappointment for herself. She'd put a lot of effort into the renovations; she'd spent a lot of time there. So had Max. What was he going to say about this?

"There's nothing else to do . . . unless you'd want to take over the project and open the shop yourself." Juliette's expression brightened at the prospect. "That's a great idea, isn't it? Then you'd be here and—"

"Juliette, I have a business. A successful insurance-investigation business. In Boston." It seemed unreal even as she said it. "All I need is a dress shop in Eureka Springs."

"But what about Max?"

"I don't think he needs a dress shop either."

"That isn't what I meant and you know it."

Sylvie did know, but she had no intention of discussing it. The difficulty of maintaining a long-distance love affair had already occurred to her, but she wouldn't have to face that decision for a while. Besides, everything might work out for the best. Somehow, it always did for Julie. "Then you've definitely decided to sell the Hannah Lee House?" she asked to keep her thoughts from the possibilities.

Wrinkling her forehead, Juliette brought her knees up and wrapped her arms around them. "Yes, as soon as the renovation is complete. Benton says it will be worth more then, and since it's going to be another few weeks before the Erikson estate is settled and the lien cleared, I may as well finish the work."

Sylvie noted the use of the singular pronoun, but didn't choose to respond. She felt a bit lonely all of a sudden—a ridiculous feeling, considering that only a few minutes earlier she'd wished Juliette would leave her alone. And after all, she wasn't losing a sister, she was gaining a reprieve from responsibility.

It was silly to mind, even for a moment, that Benton would be the one to advise, rescue, and generally worry about Juliette from now on. Sylvie didn't mind, not really, but she couldn't help feeling somewhat displaced.

"Well," she said quietly, "it's been a real experience being your partner for a couple of months, Julie."

"Now, don't worry about your investment, Sylvie. I'll pay you back. Benton says—" The phone interrupted and Juliette was off the bed and out of the room before it shrilled a second time. In a moment Sylvie heard the soft hello of lovers and then the muffled closing of a door.

Of their own accord her thoughts turned to Max. What was he doing now? she wondered. Was he thinking of her? Was he sleeping? Dreaming, maybe? A sweet remembrance teased the corner of her mouth. Max. She couldn't wait to tell him about Juliette and Benton, about the suggestion that *she* open the dress shop instead of Julie.

Yes, Sylvie thought. She couldn't wait to hear what Max would have to say about that.

It was three days before Sylvie had a chance to broach the subject to Max in private. On Monday, Juliette decided to announce her engagement to a few close friends at an impromptu luncheon. The luncheon stretched far into the afternoon and expanded to include friends who were not so close, acquaintances, and anyone else who passed within twenty feet of the restaurant. By the time Benton arrived from Fayetteville that evening, the luncheon was a full-fledged engagement party and had moved to Juliette's house. In the cramped quarters Sylvie had little opportunity to talk with Max and had to be content with his casual touch and not-so-casual smile.

On Tuesday, Juliette decided that their father should hear the wonderful news in person. Because Benton was in the middle of a trial, Sylvie was persuaded to make the trip home. Juliette, of course, couldn't go alone . . . and besides, it was a four hour drive, the perfect opportunity for quiet, sisterly talks about quiet, lovely wedding plans. Max was invited to go along, but he declined with a somber regret that hid an unrepentant grin.

The trip home was pleasant, and while there, Sylvie had time to make a few telephone inquiries about marketing Max's toys. She compiled a list of possible distributors and made notes about the information they would need. It was nothing definite, but it was a beginning. And it was something to think about while Juliette regaled family and hometown friends with *the* love story.

Still, Sylvie felt oddly restless during the overnight visit. She refused to give in to the impulse to phone Max and told herself the time away from him would help her keep things in perspective. But several hours later she acknowledged that she had no perspective. She just wanted to see Max, talk to him, touch him. When Juliette wheeled the car onto the driveway and parked late Wednesday afternoon, Sylvie walked straight to Max's house and into his arms.

"Mmm," he said, after a long and semisatisfying kiss, "either you missed me or you've decided not to buy me a Christmas present."

"How very astute, Mr. McConnell."

"Well, which is it?"

Sylvie draped her hands loosely at his nape and smiled a certain mysterious smile. "I guess you won't know that until Christmas, will you?"

Max pulled her closer and tipped up her chin with his finger. "You could find yourself in serious trouble making threats like that. Withholding presents at Christmas is a punishable offense, you know."

"You'll never be able to prove a thing."

With a slow glide of his hand over her hip Max proceeded to prove several things . . . all of which threatened her equilibrium. But he seemed unconcerned by her apparent loss of balance and simply lifted her into his arms and carried her to bed.

In the bedroom Sylvie's longing became a hunger like none she had ever known. She could almost believe it had been weeks, months even, since she'd first experienced his lovemaking, instead of a matter of days. Her hands roamed over him with an urgency she couldn't control, and Max moved with her, matching her every action. She *had* missed him, far more than was prudent, and she knew she could no more have prevented the quick flaring of desire between them than she could have stopped the sun from setting behind a distant hill.

And she didn't want to stop the mindless, burning passion of her body for his. She didn't want to lose the almost panicky, increasingly demanding sensations spinning and spinning inside her. Clothing became an inconvenience to be shed with little regard. Conscious thought became a slave to the intense pleasure of physical need. And throughout the journey, from consuming desire to fiery fulfillment, Max guided her. She never once doubted his direction, and somewhere along the way her heart became his hostage.

When the stormy reunion had receded to a calm, rather luxurious renewal of serenity, Sylvie sighed with contentment at being home and in his arms. The fleeting thought that she was not home and that her arms embraced an uncertain future was ignored, along with Max's suggestion that she tell him all about Juliette's wedding plans. Instead, she wanted to know how he'd occupied his time in her absence.

He began to tease her then with outlandish tales of adventures and misadventures. Sylvie was unimpressed and told him so, but he went on, undaunted, and eventually won her laughter as his reward. Finally, she turned the conversation toward the more serious topic of Hannah Lee House, with caution, unsure of what she wanted to say, unsure of what she hoped his reaction would be.

"Juliette's going to sell the Hannah Lee House," Sylvie said in a lighthearted voice that understated her feelings. "She wants to finish the renovation work and list it with a realtor as soon as possible."

"Are you positive she didn't tell *you* to take care of those details?"

"She's very definite these days about who will do what. And, amazing as it seems, she hasn't even asked me to open a can of paint or pick up a piece of sandpaper."

"There hasn't been time, Sylvie. Save your sigh of relief for another day."

His tone was easy, and she wondered if it had occurred to him that once Hannah Lee House went on the market, she would have no reason to stay in Eureka Springs.

"Juliette suggested I take over the project and go on with the plans we made for the dress shop."

There was a moment of quiet; her heartbeat dropped into a vast well of unnamed hopes.

"And what did you say?" he asked without a discernible change in tone.

"I told her the last thing I needed was a business so far from Boston." It sounded settled, with no chance of a change of mind, but Sylvie felt unsettled even before the words left her mouth. "Can you imagine? It would be sheer idiocy for me to open a dress shop here. What do I know about turn-of-the-century costumes and clothes from other eras? It's just not a practical idea."

"No," he agreed without hesitation.

Sylvie frowned, thinking that at least he could have taken a few seconds to agonize over his agreement. "Of course, I could learn if I wanted. And I'm sure I could make it a successful venture. But not from Boston."

"You're absolutely right." Max seemed to be fighting a yawn, and Sylvie curled closer to his side, wanting more of his attention.

"And you're absolutely no help."

"Help? What help? You just said you weren't considering the idea."

"Right." But she would have considered it in a minute if he'd shown any sign of encouragement. "It wouldn't work out." She paused, but couldn't restrain the question that pushed its way past her lips. "Would it, Max?"

His arm tightened around her and his breath was warm and titillating against her temple. "That's something I can't tell you, Sylvie Anne."

She didn't know what reaction she'd expected, but she knew for certain this wasn't it. Yet, what more could she say without sounding as if she were pleading for a verbal commitment from him? And she wasn't about to do that. It would have been nice to hear a note of disquiet in his voice, a hint of anxiety about her return to Boston, but if he chose to maintain that casual attitude, she couldn't ask him point blank if he wanted her to stay.

"Max," she whispered softly, knowing she was merely whistling in the dark. "I missed you."

His gentle kiss brushed her cheek. "I know."

Max wanted to say more. A lot more. But during the next few weeks he maintained a nonchalant and often painful silence. If he'd had any doubts about his feelings for Sylvie, they'd vanished the moment she walked freely into his arms. Love wasn't an emotion with which he had a great deal of experience, yet he recognized it just the same.

Once before, a long time ago, he'd felt like this . . . about Lynda. But it had not ended happily. He'd decided to resign his high-salaried, heavy-pressure job with a toy-manufacturing firm and do what he'd always wanted to do—make handcrafted toys. Lynda hadn't understood, and she had said so in the loudest, most incredulous manner at her command.

He could smile about it now, but it had been a long time before he'd been able to see the silver lining. Max had finally come to believe he'd expected too much. But then, so had she, and in the end the result was the same: they had each made their choice.

And now Sylvie had to choose. For the first time in their relationship he felt she wanted to ask his advice.

She was hesitant about taking over the dress shop, he knew, and he also knew it had little, if anything, to do with the responsibilities involved. Hell, she'd had those all along, anyway. He thought, hoped, it had more to do with him and whether or not he wanted her to stay in Eureka Springs. Max was well aware that nothing would please him more, but telling Sylvie would only influence a decision that had to be hers alone.

Sylvie loved him. He recognized that even if she hadn't as yet. But love was not a substitute for self-esteem. He could not be happy in the pressurized atmosphere of a big city, not even with Sylvie. He was satisfied with himself, with his toy store, and with his choice to measure success by his own standards. He had to allow Sylvie room to decide where and how she wanted to live and what successes she wanted in life. Only then he could speak to her about the future, *their* future.

And if she chose to return to Boston? Well, in that case he would have saved them both the embarrassment of breaking a verbal commitment. Unfortunately, whatever Sylvie chose, Max knew his heart was already firmly committed.

CHAPTER TEN

As each crisp December day blended into the next, Sylvie spent less and less of her time at Hannah Lee House. The restoration was nearing completion and Juliette was doing most of the remaining work herself. She didn't refuse Sylvie's offers of help, but she made it quite clear that she was capable of handling the job. Sylvie suspected it was a demonstration, largely for Benton's benefit, of the "new" Juliette; responsible, dependable, and even, occasionally, on time.

On his visits, which increased in direct proportion to the amount of time Juliette spent out of reach of a telephone, Benton displayed a keen appreciation for all the things she managed to accomplish in only a matter of hours. Sylvie had to admit a growing admiration for her future brother-in-law. He handled Juliette beautifully, and for that alone Sylvie felt the world owed him a debt of gratitude.

With the security of Benton's love and the demands of planning the wedding, Juliette grew quieter, easier to be with, and even more understanding of others. Sylvie ran through a gamut of emotions before settling into the acceptance that her free-spirited sister was no longer in need of a guardian angel.

Sylvie found it hard to believe, but at times she envied Juliette's calm, steady progress toward the future. A certain, settled future with the man she loved.

Sylvie wanted a share of that confidence to soothe her own doubts, but she simply didn't know how to obtain it. Max remained elusive on the subject of dress shops, weddings, and relationships. He talked for hours about his plans for the coming season. With only a little prompting he showed Sylvie the process of sculpting, molding, and working with the various mediums he used in toy making. He made love to her with a tenderness and depth of feeling that made her ache to pour her indecisiveness at his feet and allow him to guide her. But she didn't do that. She didn't really need to have the decision made for her; she only wanted to know how he felt before she made a choice.

The questions, pro and con, clung like a mist of fine rain to everything she did. No matter how she tried, she couldn't bring her wishes to focus on the practical rather than the romantic. And Max further confused the issue with his Christmas gift.

McKeever, the carousel horse from the toy store, was not a conventional gift. Sylvie couldn't believe Max was giving it to her, and she couldn't imagine why. When questioned, he told her not to look a gift horse in the mouth, but to rub his nose three times and make a wish. Sylvie had stroked Max's nose instead, whispered a wish, and later told him he was much better at fulfilling fantasies than McKeever could ever hope to be.

But she pondered the significance of his gift for days afterward. McKeever became a symbol of the choice she would soon have to make. In her apartment in Boston the carousel horse would be an oddity, a conversation piece admired for its singularity. In Eureka Springs the brightly painted statue became something else entirely, a wistful magic touched with the same unhurried, enchanting quaintness that formed the resort town.

She thought a lot about taking up permanent residence in Eureka Springs and the changes it would mean in her life-style. Yet, over a period of time, Sylvie realized it would mean more of a change to return to Boston and the offices of Smith-Kessler. Oddly enough, her attitude about life seemed to have altered course the moment she'd arrived in this town. She would have liked to believe that Max was the one and only reason, but she knew he wasn't. The town itself had captured her interest, and the idea of opening the dress shop was more and more appealing. She even, at times, considered that she might eventually help Max in designing clothing for his dolls.

By the week after New Year's, Sylvie knew what she wanted to do. She was willing to take a risk with the dress shop and with Max. If he was pleased, wonderful. If he wasn't, well, she'd worry about that when the time came. But some foolish corner of her heart hesitated to tell him until he gave some indication as to whether or not her decision mattered to him. With a resigned sigh Sylvie had to face the truth: she wasn't nearly as liberated as she'd thought she was.

She turned her attention and her hopes toward receiving that first and all-important response from one of the marketing firms she had contacted. Maybe that would be the breakthrough in this waiting game she and Max were playing. Maybe a business venture would provide the bonding their relationship seemed to lack.

The letter of interest from Kelco Toy Company arrived in the middle of a gray January afternoon. Sylvie read it with mingled relief and anticipation. The message was concise, restrained, but eager. She read through it twice, receiving the same impression both times: beneath the politely vague response there was definitely a hint of eagerness. The excitement of possibility carried her all the way to Max's door. He welcomed her with a kiss and a smile and accepted the letter she held out for his perusal. But his smile faded as he read, and when his eyes met hers, doubt squeezed tightly around her heart.

"What is this?" he asked.

Instinctively, she knew it was the most serious moment she had faced with Max so far, and confidence became a cottony taste in her mouth. "It's a letter from Kelco Toys. They've expressed an interest in marketing your dolls, maybe some of the other toys too."

"Why would they think *I* would be interested in their type of mass market distribution?"

"Aren't you?"

His lips tightened in a grim line. "That's not an answer, Sylvie."

"I think it is," she said, lifting her chin in defense. "If you're not interested in taking this opportunity, then there really is no point in discussing it."

"Opportunity? You see this"—he slapped the air with the letter—"as opportunity?"

She didn't know why he was angry, but she wasn't

going to back down. "Yes, Max, I do. You make beautiful dolls, wonderfully imaginative toys. Why shouldn't you—"

"Spare me the bit about sharing my talent with the world. The bottom line, Sylvie, is success, spelled out in capital letters according to your own personal alphabet. Financial success with a touch of public recognition thrown in for my ego. Or, more accurately, *your* ego."

"You're overreacting," she stated as calmly as her pounding heart would allow. "I wrote to Kelco and two other toy manufacturers because I wanted you to have a chance to test your talent and skill in a more challenging market. My God, Max, there's nothing wrong with making money or with being recognized by the public, especially when it's derived from work you enjoy doing. What's the point of creating something beautiful if no one else ever sees it?"

The letter crumpled in his fist. "I really thought you were beginning to understand, Sylvie. I thought you—" He turned away from her, his anger apparent in every move he made. "How could you have done this without asking me? And why? Did you think I was so backward, so ignorant of business matters, that I didn't *know* about distributors and marketing channels? Or did you just conclude that I needed someone to take care of the business details for me?"

"Max, you're blowing this all out of proportion."

"Am I? I don't think so. This isn't a simple misunderstanding, Sylvie. It goes a hell of a lot deeper than that. If you had had the slightest understanding of my feelings and of the things that are important to me, you wouldn't have done this. You would have known how furious I would be at your interference.

My business is none of yours. Remember, Sylvie? You told me that the first night you came to Eureka Springs. It's too bad I didn't think to reciprocate the warning. I should have known you wouldn't be able to resist trying to change me and make me 'better.' After all, now that Juliette has someone else to take care of life's little details for her, it was only logical you'd start looking for someone else who needed your expertise!"

She hadn't dreamed Max could get so angry. He'd always been casual and easygoing. Obviously, he'd been saving it up. With a cool exchange of heated stares she waited for him to back off. When he didn't, she decided to take the offensive. "Go to hell, Max."

"Do you really think I can find the way without you?"

"Actually, no. But you can forget about asking for my assistance. If I'd had any idea you were so—"

"Which is the whole point, isn't it, Sylvie? If you'd had any idea, if you'd only asked, if you'd given me the benefit of the doubt and not tried to correct what you consider a flaw in my character—"

"I wanted to help, damn you!" Suddenly, she was as angry as he, and she pushed her glasses into place to prove it. "I thought you were too involved with your work to risk putting it on the market. I thought if I made the contact and received a positive response, then it would give you the incentive to carry through with—"

"I don't *need* incentive." Max crushed the already crumpled letter in his fist and let it drop to the floor. How could she stand there defending this? Didn't she realize she'd as much as slapped him in the face? He'd thought she cared for him, but obviously she only cared about her own criterion for success. So much for believing love meant acceptance, he thought dismally. Sylvie had never accepted him for the man he was, a man who was happy with himself and who could have made her happy if only she'd looked past the end of her nose. "And I don't need you, either, Sylvie Anne. Take your business know-how home to Boston. We have a different way of looking at success here and, frankly, you just don't fit in."

Her heart pulsed painfully in her throat, but she'd die before she let him know. "I've decided to stay in Eureka Springs and open the dress shop. How do you feel about that?" It was the most important question she'd ever asked, but she hadn't intended to toss it at him in challenge.

"What difference does it make, Sylvie? You're going to do as you please, regardless of how anyone feels. But if you want my advice, forget the dress shop. You'll never find fame and fortune here. Does that clarify my opinion on the subject?"

"Perfectly. There's just one more thing." She straightened her shoulders to ward off the desolation of walking away from him. "I want you to come and get . . . that horse."

"McKeever?" Max's mouth formed a rueful frown. "Oh, no. You're going to need him now more than ever. The winter isn't over yet. There are still some cold and lonely days ahead, even for a woman who can take care of all of life's little details. Besides, a gift is a gift. I have no intention of returning the book on King Arthur you gave me, and I certainly would never part with the shirt and tie. You never know, I might need to dress for success someday."

"Good-bye, Max." Chin high, posture regal, she turned to leave. "Oh." She glanced over her shoulder. "Shall I write to Kelco informing them of their *gross* error? We certainly wouldn't want them to continue to believe you're a man worthy of interest, would we?"

It was a hateful thing to say and she hated the pride that made her say it, but at the moment pride was the only thing that stood between her and total humiliation.

"I think you've pretty well established your opinion of me, Sylvie Anne. So, for what it's worth, thanks for a . . . good time." The slur was unmistakable, even without the wink he added for effect. Sylvie experienced simultaneous impulses to slap him and to sob out a broken apology. She did neither, and she didn't allow herself the luxury of having the last word. It would have been a meaningless gesture, anyway, considering it was a little late in the game to say, "I love you."

"Juliette, *please* stop badgering me with questions." Sylvie folded a nightgown and laid it on top of the others in her suitcase. "*Nothing* happened. I've just decided to go home. The restoration work is done, Hannah Lee House is listed with a realtor, this house is rented from March until October, and the wedding plans are made. You don't need my help any longer, and I have other things I could be doing."

"Like what?"

Leave it to Juliette to ask for an impossible explanation. "I don't know. Things. What does it matter? It's time to leave, and I'm leaving."

"It isn't like you to run from a problem, Sylvie

Anne. That never solves anything, you know." Julie took the nightgown from the suitcase and shook it out. "This is mine. You must have borrowed it and forgotten to return it."

Sylvie grabbed the rose silk gown from her sister's hands. "You have one like it. Aunt Evelyn gave them to us two years ago at Christmas."

"Oh, is that when it happened?"

"I just told you, Juliette—"

"No, is that when it happened with Max?"

Sylvie sighed and walked to the dresser. "Nothing happened. How many times do I have to tell you that?"

"If nothing happened, why are you leaving? You and Max have had an argument. Admit it, Syl. I'm your sister. I understand how impossible you can be at times."

"Julie, I'm not up to this today," Sylvie warned.

Pushing the suitcase aside, Juliette made room for herself on the bed. "Did you fight about McKeever?"

"Don't be ridiculous. Why would we fight over a piece of wood?"

"It's a mystery to me, but ever since Christmas you've been moping around in a daze and I just thought—"

"I do *not* mope."

"But you've been crying."

"It's those stupid contact lenses. You know they bother my eyes."

Juliette shook her head. "I also know you left them in Boston. Come on, Sylvie. It will do you good to talk. You can't just pack up and leave."

Pausing between the lingerie and the sweater drawers, Sylvie let her hands grip the polished mahogany wood. "I appreciate what you're trying to do, Jul, but there's nothing to say. I had thought I might sell my half of the insurance-investigation firm to my partner and buy your investment in Hannah Lee House as soon as the lien is cleared, but—"

"Oh, Sylvie, please do." The bed bounced a little beneath Juliette's delight at the idea. "Benton received the legal papers releasing the lien yesterday. That has to be a good omen. You can—"

"No, I can't. It's just not . . ." Her voice trailed into abject silence. It had taken weeks of vacillating before she'd reached the conclusion it was, after all, a practical idea, and she wouldn't say it wasn't.

"I can't believe Max doesn't approve. He's in love, Sylvie. He'd buy the house for you if he thought you'd stay."

"He wouldn't, even if he could afford it. He—"

"My God, Sylvie. Max can afford to buy Hannah Lee House a dozen times over. Why, some of his Figures in History dolls have sold for thousands of dollars. And that 'piece of wood' he *gave* to you, is probably worth a fortune. Max McConnell is one of the leading artists in this state, Sylvie. People come from all over the country to buy his work. He usually travels during the winter months, giving seminars and talks and stuff. Didn't he tell you that?"

No, he hadn't. But then, Sylvie thought, she hadn't asked. A lump the size of her pride lodged in her throat and she had to swallow twice before she could answer. "Why didn't you tell me before, Juliette?"

"Before what? I thought you knew. You spent so much time with Max, how could you *not* know?"

Sylvie raked a shaky hand through her hair. No wonder Max had been so angry. She had given his pride a terrific below-the-belt punch. In all the time she'd known him, it hadn't once crossed her mind to ask about his craft except in the most technical ways. And then only when she wanted information to send to the marketing firm.

An artist? She'd recognized that on her own, she just hadn't thought anyone else had. How could she have been so stupidly blind? The first man to pursue her, to offer her friendship *and* a love relationship, and she'd insulted his intelligence, his talent, and his self-confidence.

"Sylvie?" Juliette said tentatively. "Are you okay?"

"Yes." It was an automatic response, empty of conscious thought. "But I'd better get this"—she waved her hand in meaningless gesture—"finished. If I don't pack now, I'll be late getting to Fayetteville and I'll miss the flight to Little Rock. I'll have to spend the night, there, I suppose, but . . ." The sentence faded into silence.

How could she bear to leave? But now there was no question of staying. Max would never forgive her. If she sent him roses and a written apology every day for the rest of the year, he wouldn't forget the awful things she'd said today. If she were in his place, Sylvie knew she wouldn't forgive and forget. Sometimes "I'm sorry" wasn't worth the breath required to say it. Still, she knew she had to offer one for the record.

"Juliette?" Sylvie straightened and pushed away from the mahogany dresser. "Would you mind packing the rest of these sweaters? I—I'm going to make a phone call."

"To Max?" Julie smiled encouragement and moved promptly to do as Sylvie had asked. "Good idea. Then I'll help you unpack."

A nice thought, but hardly in the realm of probability, Sylvie decided as she made her way into the front room and picked up the telephone. In a matter of seconds Max answered, and she sank onto the sofa in an agony of emotions.

"Hello?" His voice was clear and crisp, but Sylvie thought she detected a note of sadness in it.

"Max, it's Sylvie."

Silence.

"I wanted you to know I'm . . . leaving. This afternoon."

"Good-bye."

She drew a deep, steadying breath. "Max, I'm sorry. I was wrong about you, about everything."

"Yes, well, live and learn. I was wrong about you too." His pause sounded ominous. "I wish you much success, Sylvie Anne. And . . ."

She twisted the phone cord with nervous hope.

". . . good-bye."

Good-bye. Limp wristed, she replaced the receiver and stood, only to sink onto the sofa again. Ironic, she thought, that this was the first time she had allowed herself to expect more from a relationship than good-bye. But Max had left little doubt he meant this to be their one and only farewell. *Good-bye.* Such a plaintive word at times, and so final. So achingly, miserably final.

A tear slid from the corner of her eye. She lifted her glasses and brushed it away so Juliette wouldn't see. With a sigh Sylvie let the tortoiseshell frames slip back into place and stared at the carousel horse that occupied one corner of the room. She rose and stepped forward to run her hand along McKeever's polished surface. When another tear followed the path of the first, she rubbed his painted nose and wished she had brought those damned contact lenses.

CHAPTER ELEVEN

Sylvie discovered it was disconcerting to return to a place she had thought was home only to find that it no longer felt familiar. It was a little like returning from a trip to the corner market and finding that the lock on the door had been changed. The key to her Boston apartment still worked, of course, as did the key to her office. But both places felt different.

Even friends and co-workers seemed to have new interests, new activities, of which she was not a part. Although she plunged immediately into investigative work, she couldn't seem to rekindle the enthusiasm she'd once had for the job. From the morning alarm to the time she set the coffee maker at night, Sylvie felt as if she were out of sync with the rest of the world.

For the first week back she blamed her mood. Everything was her fault; she hadn't known how to express her emotions; she had been overly cautious about letting herself care too much; she'd thought she knew how to bring Max around, to make him see that she wanted to share in every facet of his life. It had all culminated in a misinterpretation of Max's character and a colossal mistake. For five entire days she moped and was as blue as a ballad sung after daybreak.

The second week her self-confidence began a steady recuperation, and she blamed Max for everything. It was his fault; he hadn't done such a great job of expressing his emotions, either; he'd hidden his feelings behind a teasing smile; he hadn't tried very hard to understand her character, and he certainly could have told her about his artistic success. There was no excuse for his attitude that she hadn't cared enough to ask, when he hadn't cared enough to tell her.

When the need to lay the blame at someone's door had passed, Sylvie accepted responsibility for her part in the misunderstanding. And it had been a misunderstanding—not as complicated as Max had indicated, but not as simple as she had thought either. Still, she had apologized, or tried to do so, and until he was willing to accept it . . . She didn't let her thoughts linger too long on what would happen if he never reached that point.

Juliette telephoned frequently with news of Benton and the wedding, Benton and the weather, Benton and the house they wanted to buy in Fayetteville, Benton and his wonderful idea about something or other. Occasionally, she tossed out Max's name to be sure Sylvie was listening, but the conversation always began and ended with an affirmation that Sylvie would be at the wedding and nothing could keep her away. Juliette seemed satisfied with the promise and didn't overload her long distance bill by repeated inquiries about Sylvie's emotional state.

Which was a good thing, considering that Sylvie didn't know from moment to moment what state her emotions were in. But it wasn't her nature to wait for something to happen. Not knowing what to do was no excuse for doing nothing, so she made a few decisions and a lot of plans.

Sylvie blinked furiously and leaned closer to the lighted mirror. Her reflection blinked back, red, teary eyes and all. Well, so much for the idea of wearing her contact lenses to the wedding. She didn't know why she'd decided to try them on. They'd never felt quite right, even after several adjustments in the prescription. She preferred anyway the sense of style and security she got from wearing her glasses.

But for some reason she'd been restless on this Friday evening, the day before she was supposed to return to Eureka Springs for the wedding. The tinted lenses played up the green of her eyes, but the effect was diminished somewhat by the irritation. She put a finger to her eyelid in preparation for removing the right lens, but paused when the doorbell rang.

With a glance at her watch she flipped off the mirror lights and made her way to the living room of her apartment. She brushed the wetness from her eyes one more time and blinked the doorknob into focus. How did people ever get used to these damned—

"Max." It was a mistake. He couldn't be standing there, looking undeniably wonderful, endearingly casual. The contact lenses were tricking her into thinking he was here. That had to be the explanation. In seconds she ran through a checklist to establish the illusion: tall, broad shouldered, blue jeans, flannel shirt and suede leather coat, brown hair, still a bit long, blue eyes, still harboring an indigo mischief, dark brows, and a special smile. But . . .

"You grew a beard." She gripped the door to stay the impulse to touch this new addition to his face. It had a soft, crinkly look, and to her surprise she liked it. A lot. "I didn't know you could do that in three weeks."

His smile slowly deepened. "You'd be surprised at the things I can do in three weeks."

"I hope I'll be surprised at the things you're going to do in the next three minutes."

His throaty chuckle rippled through her in pure sensual delight as his arms opened to invite her into his embrace. With pounding heart she accepted and lifted her lips in welcome. When his mouth settled sweetly on hers, Sylvie closed her eyes and enjoyed the crisp, wiry touch of his beard against her skin, his seductive masculine scent, the tension coiling tightly low in her stomach, and the sense of contentment she'd never known outside his arms.

When they finally moved from the doorway into the privacy of the apartment and Max had removed his coat, he cupped her chin in his hands. After another long, satisfying, and breathless kiss they settled onto the sofa cushions, as close together as she could discreetly manage to get. When Max drew back to study her face, Sylvie tried hard to control her need to blink.

"You've been crying, Sylvie Anne," he accused cautiously, as if he expected an argument. "Is there any special reason?"

"I'm practicing self-discipline."

He frowned. "Oh, I see," he said, although he didn't see at all.

"Yes, so can I, but not well. I'm wearing contacts and everything's a bit blurry." She ran her palm along one flannel sleeve, unwilling to stop touching him. "Especially your reason for being here."

"Oh, that. Well, I'm still a bit confused on the main reason myself." He lifted a hand to stroke her hair. "Officially, I'm here to make sure you arrive in time for the wedding. Juliette thought you needed an escort."

"And how hard did she have to twist your arm, Max?"

"Hardly at all. Which brings us to the unofficial reason. I came to apologize. I was wrong to lose my temper the way I did."

"I came to the same conclusion," she agreed, "about the same time I admitted to myself that I was wrong to interfere in your life the way I did."

"You've interfered in one way or another since the day you interrupted my shower."

She tilted back her head to regard him thoughtfully. "Did I ever tell you how impressed I was by your towel?"

"Never."

Her lips curved with gentle emotion. "Did I tell you I'm sorry for not understanding how you felt about your career? I never meant to insult your integrity, Max, but I saw—or thought I saw—a way to prove how much I cared for you. Unfortunately, I didn't realize there was a simpler way. You can't say I didn't warn you. Relationships are not my area of expertise."

"Oh, I don't know. You seem to be handling ours pretty well."

She shook her head in disbelief. "That's why I've spent three miserable weeks away from you, no doubt. If I learn to handle this any better, we're in big trouble."

"I love you, Sylvie." He brushed her lips with his, as if sealing a promise. "It's been a long time since I've said that to anyone, and it didn't mean the same thing to me then as it does now. Her name was Lynda and she didn't love me enough to accept the life I chose. I wanted to work with my hands, to make something that pleased me, but she couldn't understand why I would resign a promising management position with an above-average income to move to a resort town and open a small toy store. I suppose when I read the Kelco letter I was transferring some of that long-ago rejection to your motives. I wanted you to accept me and love me for *what* I did, not how successful the world thought I was."

She blinked back a sudden teary-eyed sensation that seemed unrelated to the contact lenses. "I'm inordinately proud of you, Max. I just wanted everyone else to know what a wonderful talent you have. My mistake was in not realizing everyone else *did* know."

"Well, not everyone, but enough to make me fairly successful, even by your definition."

"You should have told me you marketed your toys and dolls on a limited-edition basis." She shook her head to ward off his protest. "I know I should have thought of that possibility on my own, but your attitude was so casual about things that it simply didn't occur to me you took the business angle so seriously."

His mouth curled in a roguish smile, enhanced by the short, dark growth of beard. "I've had quite a time convincing you I could take any angle—especially *yours*—seriously."

"But you've enjoyed every minute." She tried for a demure look. "And so have I. I never knew what I was missing in life until I met you, Max. Why, I would have given ten-to-one odds against falling in love with a man who didn't own a pinstriped suit." She paused to raise her brows in question. "You don't own one, do you?"

"No, but if it's important—"

"It hasn't been important since I discovered the superiority of terry cloth."

"How do you feel about a red tuxedo?"

"Not good. How do you feel?"

"We'll find out next Friday at the wedding."

"Oh, no! Juliette told me the attendants would be dressed in red, but I didn't think she meant—"

"She meant," he said dryly. "I didn't ask where or how she was able to locate a candy-apple-red tux, complete with tails. I figured it was better not to know."

"Good thinking." Sylvie smiled with wry amusement. "We'll make quite a pair, won't we?"

"I certainly think so."

An anticipatory tingle raced clear to her toes at the loving expression in his eyes. "I love you, Max. Really. I was always afraid of letting myself care too much. It seemed like every time I started to fall in love, the relationship ended. Maybe, unconsciously, I was protecting myself, but I finally came to the conclusion I was destined to fail at love."

He pulled her closer, holding her, offering her the shelter of his love. "And now?"

"Now? Well, I have to admit I didn't intend to fall in love with you, but it happened anyway. And when we had the fight, I assumed it was the same old pattern." She pressed a kiss to the corner of his mouth in reassurance. "It didn't take too long in this empty apartment, though, before I decided I didn't have to let it happen again. I was planning to have a talk with you after the wedding, Max. I've already made arrangements to sell my half of the insurance-investigation company to Phillip and I'm buying out Juliette's investment in Hannah Lee House."

"It sounds pretty settled. What were you planning to talk to me about?"

"A problem. You see, the house next door to yours has been leased for the summer, and I thought you might consider renting a room in your house."

"Hmm. It would have to be my room, and you could only have half of the closet."

"Which half?"

"I'm versatile. You can sleep on either side."

"But what about my clothes?"

"You won't need any." His breath was warm as he began a nuzzling caress of her neck.

A slow, sweet shiver cascaded her senses and made her voice husky and uneven. "This is sounding less and less like a business agreement and more and more like a proposition, Max."

"When it sounds like a marriage proposal, you can stop me."

"Marriage? As in happily ever after?"

"None other," he said, the words muffled by his continuing caress. "Any comment?"

"Yes."

He stopped then, and raised his head to meet her eyes. The moment slipped past, and then another.

"Well?" he prompted.

"That's my comment. Yes."

"As in, I love you and will marry you and will be the mother of your children and—"

"Whoa." She placed her hand over his mouth. "Children, Max?"

He kissed her palm. "Children, Sylvie. Remember the dollhouse and the toy train? Think of it as a business arrangement. We'll have our own toy test market. A girl, a boy, and maybe—"

She put her hand back to his mouth. "The number of children we have is a negotiable point, but you shouldn't push your luck."

"How do you feel about a wedding?"

"I'm partial to a quiet, private, pre-Valentine's Day ceremony."

"What? No elaborate plans? No best man in a red tuxedo? No honor attendant in a red, heart-shaped hat?"

"Hat? Oh, no, Juliette didn't . . . ?"

He nodded solemnly. "She did. It has a feather too."

"I don't think I can stand it."

"Of course you can. By then we'll be married and you'll be so lovestruck, you won't care what you're wearing."

"I hope I won't care what you're wearing either."

"Trust me. You won't care."

With a sigh Sylvie wrapped her arms around his neck and pulled him down to lie beside her on the sofa. "This calls for a celebration. Mr. McConnell, would you care to . . . ?"

"Yes, Sylvie Anne. I would."